H.P. Lovecraft's classic tale of horror
RE-ANIMATOR

A novel by Jeff Rovin
Based on the screenplay by Dennis Paoli,
William J. Norris and Stuart Gordon

Encyclopocalypse Publications
www.encyclopocalypse.com

Contents

Chapter 1   5

Chapter 2   21

Chapter 3   41

Chapter 4   57

Chapter 5   69

Chapter 6   81

Chapter 7   89

Chapter 8   105

Chapter 9   121

Chapter 10   137

Chapter 11   149

Chapter 12   163

Chapter 13   187

Chapter 1

The sounds of Zurich bothered Herbert West as never before. It was only slightly worse than usual; he knew it was him - the experiment - and not the city itself. But it distracted him just the same.

He took the bottle from the refrigerator, held it to the bank of fluorescent lights.

"No separation," he said. "It looks good."

"Fine," replied the only other person in the room, an elderly man in a lab jacket. He resumed his writing while West fetched a syringe from the cabinet.

Noise had always bothered him. Distracted him. West remembered vividly when he was a child and there was a TV in his home in Canada. Westerns. Soap operas. Game shows. Bad enough to be distracted by noise, but to be distracted by idiocy... He recalled how glad he had felt letting his parents' executors sell it and give him the money. It was one of the few things that hadn't been lost in the early morning fire. The chemical fire. But his joy was short lived. He quickly became distressed at the levels of noise generated by the kids at the foster home in Gananoque and, later, the hoots of derelicts and the melee of traffic in New York. It seemed that for all his life he'd been trying to measure out a powder or cut away some tissue only to have someone do something loud to distract him.

Then he'd come to Zurich. The city had been a refreshing change of pace, much quieter - or at least more consistent - than anywhere he'd ever lived; rarely in the last three years had he found himself wishing for a cave in the wilderness, a place away from civilization.

Until tonight.

The Montreux Jazz Festival had brought crowds of people to the city, and they had all apparently chosen tonight to go shopping. Across the green, at Karmgasse 26, J. Otto Scherer's antique clocks went off in unison every fifteen minutes, drawing ever more pedestrians to the shop; below, a small jazz band raised a din for people taking in the warm summer night.

Maybe it wasn't *much* louder, he had to admit.

Maybe the problem was with him.

Even as he pushed the hypodermic needle through the test tube's rubber stopper and into the syrupy yellow liquid, Herbert West had mixed emotions about the experiment.

The dominant feeling, of course, was elation. He hadn't felt this good about a formula since the exquisite compound he'd developed for his meddling roommate, Joe, at the foster home. That one hadn't been as spectacular, of course. It was only a variation on a mosquito repellent suppository used by the military; a reformulation that turned Joe's semen green and left him dateless for years.

This was more important, and not just to science.

It was the culmination of seven years of dreaming, four of them fumbling blindly, on his own, at NYU, and three working with a master.

The four years at New York University still rankled him. He'd known in the first six months that the school was wrong for him, but he stayed because they'd given him a scholarship and he was able to use the labs. After having other kids at the foster home tamper with his chemicals and equipment for five years, the freedom of the university lab was intoxicating. That is, until he began discussing his work with his professors.

They'd encouraged him when he began experimenting with the magnetic field of the human brain, suggesting that it could be used to pinpoint epileptic seizures, monitor brain swelling.

Even keep it from dying.

That's when the wolves descended.

West freely expressed his growing doubt about the inevitability of death, earning him the scorn of professors and fellow students alike. He insisted that, in theory, it should be possible to create a living fossil, an exact copy of a cell which replaced the original and continued its functions. On his own, he was able to create a very elastic copy of very simple cells -but the problem was, they weren't alive. And no one would set aside the time or money to help him in his research.

West complained about the scientific community's narrow-mindedness in a letter to *Science News*, which only made things worse; fortunately, Hans Gruber had seen the letter and sent for him.

Now, three years later, they were finally going to *do* it, and West found the prospects of triumph exhilarating. After the countless hours he'd spent huddled over beakers and microscopes, studying computer terminals and contemplating the wired limbs and chemically treated organs of shrews and dogs and, of late, more and more humanlike animals, he could taste success.

Even so, as the moment neared, there were doubts nagging and profound doubts.

The doubts had nothing to do with the danger to Professor Gruber. Ever since West had joined the project three years before, they knew that one of them would have to do this, someone who could communicate exactly what was going on - how the dextroamphetamine sulphate was affecting the nervous system, whether the fluphenazine hydrochloride was doing the job for shock, if the next batch should have more or less prochlorperazine for nausea.

It had to be one of them. With his sight already failing, his hands were not quite as steady as when he'd won the Nobel Prize for chemistry twenty years earlier, Gruber had known that West was the man for the job. Now he was calm and ready. Seated on a stool by the jab bench, he was quietly savoring the moment in his own way, carefully spooning powders from a series of dark brown bottles and collecting them in a petri dish. West admired his professional detachment more than he could say and only hoped that his mentor would be present to collect his second Nobel Prize.

The young man's eyes narrowed, his thick brows folding over the tops of his eyeglasses. He studied the hypodermic carefully as the fluid climbed slowly into the barrel. He was tempted for a moment to stop at 15 cc's. They'd asked two different computer programs for suggested dosages based on the results of the gibbon test. Adjusted to Gruber's own system, both programs came up with 15 cc's. However, after doing an autopsy on the ape and finding that the drug hadn't saturated the thyroid gland and the lungs, Gruber had overruled the machines and decided to go with 25 cc's. West didn't agree, but Gruber had overruled him as well. *"Better to overkill than to kill-over,"* he'd joked. In any case, the question of who was right would be answered soon enough.

8

West had his doubts about the undertaking, not because of anything they were about to do; the experiment was absolutely necessary. He worried because if anything were to happen to Gruber he'd be alone... utterly alone. True, he'd done much of the research by himself while Gruber lectured in Switzerland and abroad, collecting hefty speaker's fees which helped to pay for expensive materials they couldn't justify billing to the university - like the two-toed sloth and the tar gibbon to test versions of the formula. The blind eye Dr. Willett turned to their work precluded any direct support. But the professor was always available with a helpful insight, a learned supposition, an inspired reformulation.

And Gruber had always called him Herbert or Mr. West. He didn't have to be told or corrected, he'd sensed not to call him by a nickname from the start. He was a man of rare perceptions, and he deserved nothing less than sainthood. Unlike with most saints, however, West wanted him canonized while he was alive.

His impassive expression changing, West grinned as the fluid reached the 25cc scale marking. The serum would work, they would publish and become famous, and - when their time came - not a soul from the foster home or the school or from Toronto and the Maple Leaves would get any of it.

Not a drop for them, West thought with some delight. He'd use it on another gibbon before he'd give it to the people who had made his life so unpleasant, so needlessly unfruitful.

Gruber looked back, his flesh taut over his bony face. "Are we ready, Mr. West?"

The young man slid the test tube into its rack and brought the hypodermic close to his thick glasses. The measurement was precise, the needle cannula was clear.

"Yes, sir. We're ready."

"Excellent."

The large eyes of the elderly biochemist were solemn beneath the burst of white hair that hung over his forehead and back along his ears. The tall, lanky man weakly brushed the tangle from his brow and gazed at his lap. After a moment, he said in his thick German accent, "They scream when they're born, and they scream when they die!"

West looked at him curiously. "Sir?"

"Strindberg," explained the professor. "From *A Dream Play*." He looked back at the small mound of powders. "What do *you* think, Mr. West? Will we add a new dimension to the playwright's line? Will I scream when I am reborn?"

The slender young man frowned and slid one hand into the pocket of his lab jacket. "That depends, sir. If you're wrong about the extra 10 cc's and there's a buildup in the neuromuscular junctions-"

The professor interrupted with a slow wave of his hand. "I did not mean for you to take me *literally*, Mr. West. I was speaking about my soul. How will God respond to what we are about to do?"

The rebuke stung, but West didn't let it show. He never claimed to be a scholar, he was a scientist. And from that sixth-grade science project, when he had kept a mouse alive for over a day using a quarter-pint of his own blood, he had resolved to be nothing more or less than the greatest biochemist since Pasteur.

"God should be delighted," West replied. "After all, he hasn't seen anything like this for nearly two thousand years."

The professor snickered. "You know, Mr. West, you give me hope... you truly do. Whatever hap-pens to me, you *will* make this project succeed. People who are unconstrained by propriety have

10

always made the most effective scientists."

This comment, too, West allowed to pass. Gruber always became a humanist when they were about to reach for a new plateau in their work. He had come to recognize it as the old man's way of hedging against failure, of reminding himself and others that he was not a superman. West filled with fresh anticipation as he wondered if these ephemeral, nonbiological traits would survive the experiment.

The young scientist also felt a sudden bubbling in his stomach. He looked at the wizened man and then at the syringe.

"Professor," West said, "there's something I wanted to say to you."

"Yes, Mr. West?"

"You *do* know how I feel, don't you?"

"About the experiment?"

"No, sir. About you."

Gruber seemed pleased. He rubbed his knees. "I have my suspicions, Mr. West, but it would do my soul good to hear them - and yours good to say them, I think."

West was clearly uncomfortable. "You've been like a father to me," he said. "Whatever happens, I want you to know that I appreciate all you've done."

"Appreciate." Gruber played with his chin. "A rather mild word from some, but a serious confession when it comes from Herbert West." He smiled.

"I shouldn't tease you, should I? In three years, I don't think I've ever told you that I love you like a son, and have taken a pride in your achievements that I never thought I would experience."

Gruber was not surprised to see how uncomfortable the praise made West feel. He was not a young man who knew how to give or take anything that was non-intellectual, could not be weighed on a scale or measured using hashmarks on a beaker. But one day, perhaps, the moment they'd shared here would mean something. Maybe one day. In that respect, he wasn't much different from Hill, whom he had caused to resign four years before for his shocking lack of ethics. Gruber only hoped that if something went wrong and he did not recover, his young associate would have the good sense, if not the charity, at least to stay within the law.

With a reassuring smile, the old man closed his thin lips over the spoon. He took the mixture down in a single gulp, and, almost at once, the compound went to work. The cocaine overdose shut down his heart, and with a small gasp he slumped over the bench; he was oblivious to the cyanide as it went to work on his bloodstream or the Acidulin as it generated enough gastric juices to eat through his stomach lining.

Gruber dropped from the bench to the floor, landing on his face with a loud slap. West hurried over and flipped him onto his back, pulling a stethoscope from his lab coat.

"August 24, ten-thirty P.M.," he said evenly as he placed the instrument to Gruber's chest, deftly pulling the binaurals around his head with one hand while holding the syringe, needle up, in the other.

"Professor Gruber's heart has stopped, and I expect the ingestion has also affected his circulatory system and stomach as we anticipated." Tossing the stethoscope aside, he switched the hypodermic to his right hand and put it to Gruber's hairless chest. "About to inject 25cc's of serum, which we've calculated will counteract the poisons and restore the professor's dead tissue."

Jabbing the needle into Gruber's flesh, West pushed the plunger until he'd emptied the barrel, then sat back on his heels to await the results; the wait was not a long one.

Down the corridor, Dr. Margot Koslik was singing softly as she studied a tumor section under a microscope.

"Den atem des lebens hauchte er in sein angesicht-"

When she heard the scream, the portly radiologist snapped off the rest of Haydn's *Creation* and stood with her ear cocked toward the corridor. The scream came again, louder than before.

"Professor Gruber?"

Of course, it was Gruber, she told herself. He and his assistant were the only other people in the building, and Margot couldn't imagine young West screaming.

"Nothing affects him," she complained. Not a pretty girl's smile or the triumphs of a hardworking colleague. Between the short-cropped black hair and expressionless mouth, his cold blue eyes were perennially slit and staring, focused on something only he could see.

Yes, the scream had to have come from Gruber. But if he were ill or had hurt himself, why hadn't West come out to call for help? She hesitated to go over, not wanting to get into a debate with West over why she was interfering, why she wasn't minding her own business. Falling into his mouth was an experience not even Dr. Willett enjoyed. If only the little bastard hadn't had Gruber's protection.

"Fuck him," she decided.

The short woman rose from her stool and waddled past a shelf full of jarred organs. She poked her head into the dark hallway. Three rooms down on the opposite side, she saw hazy shadows moving violently across the bright, frosted glass of the door. She took a few steps toward it.

"Herr Professor?"

A third scream echoed from the room, followed by a low gurgling and the hollow thud of stomping feet; beneath these she heard West mumbling in his clipped, mechanical voice.

"Professor, are you all right?"

Another scream was followed by the shattering of glass, and, with a small oath, Margot spun and hurried toward the phone.

The police car swung into the parking lot just as Dr. Willett was climbing from his Audi. He stood rigid, impatiently tapping his toe as the two officers jogged over. This was all he needed, a scientific misadventure at the Institute. It would be the worst disaster to befall the local medical community since Mary Shelley had opted to make Victor Frankenstein Swiss. The three men entered the ivy-covered building together.

"Did she actually enter the room?" asked one officer as they walked briskly down the corridor.

"I'm aware of nothing more than I told you over the phone," Willett lied in clipped, unpleasant tones. Willett had known what Gruber was up to, and that was what worried him. He'd let the professor use the facility because widespread honors and lavish grants would be accorded the Institute were he to succeed, and Gruber had *promised*, sworn absolutely to stick to animals.

Of course, that was before West had joined the project.

Things had moved along faster since Gruber had rescued West from the Neanderthal minds and Hunnish souls at NYU. Using Gruber's research, West had made that all-important breakthrough of stimulating the chromatin in the dead rat and reactivating mitosis. Since then, he'd managed to bring entire animals back for limited stays, though each of them died soon thereafter because West was unable to pinpoint quickly enough what was failing and why. Willett shut his eyes and exhaled weakly; he could taste his lobster dinner in his throat. He'd been the youngest man ever appointed to this position at the university and did not intend to be the first man in the school's long history to have to resign the job. As he heard the faint snarls echoing down the tiled corridor, he prayed fervently that Gruber had mere-ly had a heart attack or spilled acid on himself.

As they rounded the corner, their footsteps drew Margot around. She'd been pacing anxiously before room 121, and now she held her hands toward it in a gesture of hopelessness.

"Has anything else happened?" Willett demanded, nervously tugging at the knot of his tie as he stopped beside the radiologist.

"Nothing, Herr Doctor. Only these horrible noises and... now and then a scream."

Emboldened by the presence of the police officers, Margot narrowed her eyes and slid around Willett. After seven P.M. this was her responsibility, her domain. She rapped several times on the door.

"Professor Gruber!"

There was more muttering and then another loud shriek.

"Herr Professor!"

Perspiration forming on his brow, Willett stepped forward and put his mouth close to the door.

"Hans! Herr West!"

The dull thumping of shoes against the tiles punctuated the low, guttural sounds coming from within. "Let us in!" Willett shouted. "Open the door at once!"

There was another scream, followed by

something unintelligible from West. Licking his lips, Willett nodded at the police officers and stepped back as one used his nightstick to break the pane directly above the knob, the other reaching in and opening the door. The officers drew their guns and rushed in, followed by Willett and Margot; what they saw caused them all to stop dead in the doorway.

Professor Gruber was writhing horribly on the floor, his features contorted and white. His gnarled fingers clawed at the floor; his legs and heels jumped up and down as though they were being pumped with electricity. Kneeling beside him, looking back at the newcomers, West had an empty syringe in his hand and a grim expression on his face. Like a child who'd been caught with his hand in the cookie jar, he let the hypodermic fall as his expression shaded to shock.

"I - *we* need to be left alone," he said flatly. Then, reaching for the stethoscope and slipping it around his neck, he turned back toward the professor.

His eyes ablaze, Willett finally raised a trembling finger and pointed toward the youth. "Get him out of here."

Scowling from the tart fumes which filled the laboratory, the two officers hustled over and, grabbing West under his arms, yanked him to his feet. He squirmed away from them and bent back down over the professor.

"You idiots, you don't understand! I have to record his vital signs!"

The blue-suited men pulled him roughly from the scientist's side, dragging him back toward the door amidst his shrill protests. Ignoring West, Margot strode toward the contorting old man.

"Professor, can we help you? What is wrong?"

"Only *I* can help him!" West shouted. "Let me *go*, fools!"

16

Thinking the professor might be having an epileptic seizure, Margot plucked a pencil from her vest pocket. Leaning forward to place it between his teeth, she screamed when the lanky scientist shot suddenly to his feet. Streams of yellowish spittle began pouring from the sides of his mouth, and his eyes bulged unnaturally. His high-pitched scream spoke of agonies the others couldn't begin to comprehend.

Wrestling himself from the constables, West pushed past the radiologist and grabbed the professor.

"Sir, what is it? *Where* is it?"

West went to press the diaphragm of the stethoscope to his chest but stepped back when he felt something hot spray against his belly. He looked down and saw the professor's hands clasped to his midsection. Greenish liquid was shooting from between his fingers - his gastric juices eating right through his body. Obviously, the formula had overcompensated for the cyanide but under-compensated for the Acidulin; he should have given the injection lower in the chest to balance the absorption.

The officers came forward again but froze when the professor's brow and eyes began to throb and crawl. He began to claw at his temple, raking long bloody lines in the soft flesh. His lids began to tear as the eyeballs bugged even further, blood seeping out from around them. Suddenly, the right eye exploded, showering blood on Margot and West. The woman screamed and backed into the arms of the startled Willett; West simply stared in fascination.

The brain took in too much blood and is hemorrhaging, he concluded. Gruber was wrong after all. The extra .5 cc's had been soaked up entirely by the brain, which drew not only the blood but the formula *in* that blood back to it. That would also explain the presence of the formula in his saliva.

Gruber's other eye burst, blood spilling forth and also gushing from a gash on the forehead he'd suffered when he first hit the floor. Gurgling horribly, he crumpled at Willett's feet; then he was still. The room was silent for a long moment. Taking a deep breath, Willett stepped gingerly across the blood-spattered tiles and lifted his colleague's wrist.

"He's dead."

"Of course he's dead," West sneered. "The dosage was too large."

Margot looked over, her mouth hard. "You killed him. You killed Professor Gruber!"

"No," he gently corrected her, "I did not kill him."

West's features were impassive as he looked from the corpse to the woman. Glancing back at the body, he proudly announced, "To the contrary. I *gave* him life!"

The inquest was brief, and, by making deals with families who wanted their children to one day go to medical school, Willett was able to keep press coverage to a minimum.

Although West was exonerated, he decided to leave Switzerland all the same. Anything he did there would meet with stern resistance from Willett and intruding eyes from the authorities, and he simply couldn't work in that kind of Orwellian climate. He needed someplace smaller, more anonymous. A school without a reputation but with a good deal of money, the kind of institution one found in the U.S., in towns where large corporations tried to look good by endowing small schools.

After making a thorough study of the situation, he decided to go against Gruber's wishes and apply to Miskatonic in Arkham, Massachusetts. That would fit the bill on both counts. As he recalled hearing at NYU, Ogan Chemical had founded the school several years before, the same year it had poisoned the river. The press was a wash, and the river was eventually cleaned up. But the medical school and hospital remained, gems in the Ogan crown.

West had no doubt that he'd be accepted and that the money Gruber had left him would cover his tuition and allow him to continue their research in solitude.

However, there was another reason for applying to Miskatonic. The reason Gruber had told him to stay away. A reason nearly as compelling as the others.

Carl Hill practiced there.

West wasn't sure whether Gruber had warned him away because he feared what Hill would do to him or what he would do to Gruber. No matter. He had long wanted to meet him, to see firsthand what an antiscientist looked like, a man not interested in the ecstasy of science but in its profits. A man who had not only crossed Professor Gruber but had the utter audacity to paraphrase Gruber's private notebooks and publish them as his own.

West would miss Gruber, but going to Miskatonic would soften the blow. For the first time since he had sat at the kitchen table and watched his family fall apart, Herbert West felt free. *Purpose* had freed him.

As he dashed off a letter to Miskatonic, he couldn't help but wonder for which accomplishment the scientific community would eventually thank him more; ridding the earth of death or putting an end to the career of Dr. Carl Hill.

Chapter 2

Lean and rangy with eyes like machines, Carl Josiah Hill took breakfast on his balcony while he scanned the morning paper. The Miskatonic Ledger was only a local tabloid, but he enjoyed seeing his name in headline type. Today, of course, it was only on page six - a lengthy item about the grant and a novice's inaccurate summary about the powers of the laser drill. But one day it would be page one, and not just in Miskatonic. He'd come up with something that would make headlines the world over and win him every accolade the scientific community could thrust on him. The drill was a good start. With it, he could search more thoroughly and efficiently for the human soul. He had always sworn he'd find it, conclusively, before he was fifty. He had eight years to go, more than enough time. With Dean Halsey in his back pocket and his work bringing distinction to the medical school, it was only a matter of time.

The wind disturbed his gray hair, and he turned slightly so it would blow front to back rather than side to side. He took a bite of dry wholewheat toast and a sip of coffee. He shook his head.

Hill had taken the pains to explain the instrument carefully, yet the report was still a shambles. He'd said the beam could hypothetically drill through teeth, but he hadn't said it could be used for dentistry. It would melt fillings and burn through the gum or cheek if the dentist slipped. He'd made a point of explaining how the instrument improved medicine by limiting the amount of blood spilled and thus allowing the surgeon a better view of the diseased area. He'd never said anything about it being painless, which it wasn't, yet there it was in the quotes. And she had made the purely sloppy error of using the verb "to laze" instead of "to lase." She lazed, he lazed how could she confuse the two?

At least she'd spelled his name right. Shaking his head, he took some consolation in the fact that he'd been right about her. He knew as soon as she opened her mouth that reporter Phyllis Freeman would not understand. He'd gone on about the drill's operation for one reason only: he'd wanted her to find him fascinating.

The sliding door opened behind him. Hill didn't bother turning.

"Good morning, my dear. Sleep well?"

The young woman stretched, sucked in the morning air. "That's a terrific waterbed you have. I love it."

That wasn't what he'd wanted to hear. She'd seemed to enjoy their lovemaking; was she as dead below the waist as above the shoulders?

She leaned over him, draping her arms over his chest. "Uh-oh. There it is."

He was glad she could read. He was beginning to wonder.

"So, Dr. Hill. What did you think?"

A barge hooted on the river several stories below; the timing was perfect.

"I think," he said, craning around, admiring

the depth of the cleavage in his too-large bathrobe, "that you are a lovely writer."

The pert young woman smiled and kissed him on the cheek.

"Thank you!"

As he suspected, she hadn't listened to that either. He hadn't said that she wrote lovely prose or that she was even an adequate writer. He'd simply told her that she was lovely, which was the truth.

He patted her hand. "Now why don't you go into the kitchen and get yourself some breakfast? There is bacon draining on the paper towels and hardboiled eggs in the refrigerator. You *do* know how to peel the shells-"

She tapped him on the head. "Of course, silly."

Silly, he thought as she walked away. The last person who'd called him silly was his niece, and she was seven. It was either a firm young body and a limp mind or a mature mind and a less than firm body. Why could he rarely find both? Even the women he paid for were rarely ideal. The escort service trained them to listen; that was as important to their success as staying in shape. In truth, the women were just like bad psychiatrists, only pretending to listen while he talked his problems out.

Then, of course, there was Megan. God, was there Megan.

Beautiful and spirited, she was not the brightest girl in the world, but she had potential. More, she had lips that turned his loins to soup. And grace. A product of the finest prep schools, she was more poised and confident than any woman he had known, a goddess in need of only one thing: a god. He shook off his reverie. There wasn't time to get Phyllis back into bed, so he took a bite of egg and returned to the newspaper. A small item in "Comings and Goings" caught his eye and quickly pushed Megan from his mind. He read it with mounting distress.

"And a warm, hands across the border welcome to Herbert West," it read. "Formerly of Toronto, New York, and Zurich, Mr. West will be arriving in Arkham today to begin his studies at Miskatonic. The winner of the 1977 Young Scientists of Canada Gold Medal for his work in electrical rejuvenation of dead animal tissue, he was most recently a student aide to the late Nobel Prize winner Hans Gruber at the University of Zurich. Dean Allan Halsey of Miskatonic told us, 'We are delighted to have a student of Mr. West's caliber join our student body, and trust that Arkham will help him feel right at home.' "

Hill's hands dropped, crushing the paper in his lap. He stared across the river, over the old homes and spires of Arkham.

"It can't be," he said. "Why didn't Allan discuss this with me?"

Dean Halsey hadn't told him, he decided, because Halsey was a shortsighted ass. West was just another prize catch, another potential grant getter. He probably hadn't analyzed it any deeper than that.

"Dr. Hill, do you have any Pine Sol or something? I kind of smashed an egg on your counter."

He shut his eyes, mumbled for her to leave it, the housekeeper would be there soon. He thought of Halsey's stupidity, did some deep breathing to try and stay calm. How a fool like Halsey could have fathered a woman like Megan was a mystery to him. He thought about Herbert West. The name was unfamiliar to him, but West had to be good. If he weren't, Gruber would never have taken him on. What's more, he had to be coming to Miskatonic for a reason. This wasn't the kind of school to which someone transferred by chance. The

24

tuition was far in excess of its prestige, catering mainly to wealthy Massachusetts families with an occasional scholarship thrown in to keep the government happy. With his credentials, West could have been accepted to any number of schools. He was coming for a reason, and Hill had a good idea what that reason was: him. The question was, did he simply want to study with him, with a former colleague of Professor Gruber or was he after something else?

He continued shallow breathing for several moments more and then opened his eyes. He was being premature and paranoid, had slept too little, and was thinking too much. He returned to his meal.

Phyllis came onto the terrace with her breakfast tray and began prattling about what a magnificent view he had and how her own apartment looked out on an Ogan Chemical sewage processing facility.

Hill didn't even make a pretense of listening. He wanted to finish breakfast and get over to the university, to take a look at the newcomer's file. Though science surprised him constantly, people did not; that was one reason he prospered and published while his colleagues went unrecognized. Why photodynamic therapist Douglas Scott had been unable get his laser surgery ideas off the ground until Hill had taken him under his wing.

Why Herbert West would be his ally or be out on his ear, his future in ruins.

A cloud passed across the sun, throwing a chill into the warm October morning. Phyllis pulled the robe tighter, but Hill barely noticed her or the drop in temperature. Rising, he told the girl to dress and did likewise; fifteen minutes later she was standing at the bus stop while he raced his Jaguar toward the school.

Dr. Grace Harrod cursed as she left one corpse, a young man who had shot himself in the head, and ran to what the odds said was about to be another. She had complained often to the hospital board about conditions in her emergency room, about how they were constantly getting overflow from Springfield's understaffed John F. Kennedy Memorial Hospital, and how that overflow was straining their own facilities. But no one seemed to care. The board refused to give her more staff or even to lodge a complaint with the Kennedy board. They liked being what Halsey had called "The Little Engine That Could" of hospitals. It kept up morale, he said, and - though he didn't say this - Harrod knew it also made Ogan Chemical look good. The hospital the firm had endowed was all that stood between health and utter chaos, which was great for the corporate image.

It didn't seem to matter to anyone that the lack of personnel cost them a life now and then. As long as the bottom line looked good and the press was favorable, nothing was going to change. Nothing like the two extra minutes this poor young girl had had to wait before they could unload the ambulance and send it out again.

The ER medical director entered cubicle 3 and stood back while her staff prepped the body.

"What's the story?"

Intern Judie Reynolds filled her in. "Heart attack, no vital signs."

"I heard someone say she had to wait-"

"We went out two minutes after the call came in. Got her here in three. She'd already lost everything by the time we got there."

"Shit."

Five minutes without oxygen; even if they brought her back, they might not bring all of her back.

"All right, I'm going to zap her."

Dr. Harrod half turned from the side of the unconscious woman and reached for the defibrillator paddles. To her left, one nurse was compressing an ambu-bag to feed the patient oxygen while, behind her, another monitored her vital signs. The green line on the electrocardiogram was straight and unpromising.

"C'mon, charge 'em! Let's go, let's go!"

One young intern apologized while another squeezed conductive gel onto the paddles. Her lips tightly pursed, Dr. Harrod pushed the metal plates together to spread the gel evenly.

Damn Allan Halsey, she thought. She couldn't believe she'd actually considered marrying him when she first came to Miskatonic from UCLA. She'd realized later that it was Megan she felt sorry for. She still did. Life with Halsey could not be easy. While she stepped over to the patient, whose death was written in the pallor of her face, Harrod reminded herself that she'd given up Los Angeles for this, had run from the bloody street crime and drug overdoses that never seemed to quit to the quiet suburban setting of Arkham. If she'd known that red tape and bullshit could be as frustrating as failed law enforcement and drug rehabilitation programs, she might never have come. As it was, she couldn't leave now because she knew that if she did, the whole system would unravel. That's what had happened when the previous medical director left, and she couldn't live with herself if she put the city and her interns through that kind of hell.

Of course, every now and then there were compensations like the young intern across the table. Daniel Cain had his hands folded one on top of the other on the patient's bare chest, administering cardiopulmonary resuscitation. He stepped back when Harrod approached. Cain was naive but an excellent

27

diagnostician with a superb bedside manner. If he managed to come down from his idealistic ivory tower, he'd make a fine physician. If not, he'd end up running from the very imperfect medical establishment and treating yokels in the backwoods of New Hampshire.

The doctor placed the charged rectangular paddles on the woman's chest and pressed the triggers. The patient's limbs jerked, stiffened, then fell back.

Standing beside the monitor, Judie Reynolds shook her head gravely.

"Straight line."

Dr. Harrod looked over at Charles Ward, who was squeezing the air bag.

"Anything?"

"Nada."

"I'm going to zap her again."

The process was repeated, and once again the results were negative. Dr. Harrod rose from the body.

"All right, let's call it."

"No!" Cain placed his strong hands between the patient's breasts, resuming the external massage.

Dr. Harrod shot him a stern look. "Mr. Cain, I *said* give it up."

He continued pressing down with slow, firm strokes. "She just needs a little more time. The drugs have to circulate."

"The drugs? We just gave her two shots of forty volts!"

Ward quipped, "That's enough to jump start a 747."

"We don't need her to fly," Cain said humorlessly, "just to live."

"We've done everything that can be done for this woman," Dr. Harrod continued, "and she's not going to respond. She's *gone*."

Cain looked up from the body. Dr. Harrod's

eyes were hard, the expressions of the three other interns dispassionate as they replaced the equipment and swabbed the decks for the next slab of meat. Reluctantly, he backed away.

The seasoned resident shook her head. "Cain, your optimism is touching but a waste of time. A good doctor knows when to stop."

"I'm sorry, Dr. Harrod, I was just-"

"Wasting time on a dead woman when there are patients in this hospital who need us." Her eyes softened. "Look, I've said it before, and so has Dean Halsey: you're one of the most dedicated young doctors I've ever worked with. But you *do* have to accept, Cain, that once six minutes have passed, it's better to let them be."

Ward sang out softly, "Brain damage... malpractice!"

The rattle of the wheels in the corridor pulled the resident and her interns around. "Accident on I-95!" shouted an orderly as he raced past with a blood-soaked stretcher. "Make room, there's two more coming!"

Dr. Harrod bolted for the door. "Ward, Reynolds, Trupin - you come with me. Cain, you take Ms. Grant to the morgue."

After watching his colleagues dash down the hallway into another cubicle, Cain dragged his perspiring palms down the front of his green robe, pushed his longish brown hair from his eyes, then ambled over and pulled a tag from a drawer. Printing the young woman's name on it, he slipped the tag on a toe, drew the sheet over her head, and wheeled the table toward the elevator.

Harrod's logic be damned, this was the most upsetting loss he'd experienced in some time. The young woman's name was Wendy Grant, and she'd suffered cardiac arrest while leading an aerobics class. From what sketchy details they'd been given, she had no history of heart disease or circulatory problems. In the three years he'd been at the Miskatonic Medical Center, Cain had lost car-crash victims, a few junkies, and a lot of overweight smokers. This one hurt because the woman wasn't as far gone as most. There should have been *something* they could do to save her.

Cain wondered again if he'd survive his internship. It wasn't going days without sleep that got to him, or having to work with Dr. Harrod, who had the patience of a tiger shark. It wasn't even that idiot Ward, who spent far less time healing the sick than he did blowing grass and thinking up clever nicknames to go with Cain, like "Nova" and "Coe" and "Candy."

What troubled him was losing far more patients than he saved. That wasn't the way he always thought it would be.

For as long as he could remember, Cain had wanted to work in a hospital emergency room rather than have a private practice or do research. His father was a storefront lawyer dedicated to helping the impoverished in Washington, D.C., and even now Cain loved nothing more than to listen to him talk about this cause he was championing or that eviction he'd gotten the courts to rescind. Truly a son of the sixties, Cain had taken up medicine to help people. He'd come to Miskatonic from Johns Hopkins because, only five years old, it was as complete and modern a facility as a doctor could wish for. And as a traffic cop he was fine, mending broken bones or suturing cuts with skill and good humor. But as a marksman, getting in there and gunning down the big ailments, he wasn't nearly the crack shot he'd always dreamed of being. No one was, but the dream was dying hard.

Cain rode the elevator to the basement and

headed for the morgue. As usual, big Mace was holding down the fort. Seated behind his desk in the hallway, he was rolling a cigar around his mouth while he read the newspaper. The former college tackle looked up when he heard the squeaking of the wheels. He grinned broadly.

"Hey, Cain! How goes it?"

The intern smiled weakly. "I've had better mornings." He stopped beside the heavy metal door. "Got another one for ya."

"So I noticed. Ain't locked, though. Dr. Hill's in the autopsy room." Mace chuckled. "Don't know why they keep locked doors around here in the first place. Nobody wants in, and there ain't nobody gettin' out."

"Insurance," he replied. "A body was stolen out from under your predecessor's nose, and the family sued the hell out of us."

"Probably did it themselves," Mace commented as he returned to his paper.

Opening the double doors, Cain backed the table into the cavernous cinderblock room. He pushed it along slowly, so as not to distract Dr. Hill and his assistant, Douglas Scott. The two men were huddled beneath a single bright spotlight in the center of the room. Hill was using a laser to open a small hole in a cadaver's forehead, just above the right eye. A tenuous stream of smoke rose from the burning flesh, the smell of which was strong enough to overpower even the antiseptic odor that pervaded the chamber.

Putting his back to a heavy metal door marked "Restricted Area," Cain pulled the table inside. The sweat on the front of his smock grew cold in the refrigerated air, and Cain shivered as he looked around.

"Great."

The small room was full, tables packed side by side along the green-tiled walls. But he wouldn't leave Ms. Grant in the aisle; although she'd had no dignity in dying, she would have a measure of it in death.

Jockeying the carts nearest him closer together, Cain managed to squeeze out enough room for the new arrival. While sliding her in, he accidentally nudged the table to her left; the arm of the other corpse rolled from beneath its sheet, swinging grotesquely in the narrow space between the tables. Cain reached out and replaced it, the flesh cold and stiff. The first time he'd handled a cadaver, the skin had reminded him of a milk carton; from that point on he'd had to get all his calcium from pills, since he was no longer able to keep milk down.

Dr. Hill seemed not to notice Cain when he returned to the autopsy room. The gaunt Hill was a strange sort. Fortyish, with a long face and hollow eyes that made him look older, the neurosurgeon had earned his reputation in the early seventies, having been the first to apply computers to a complete study of brain death. During the course of his research at the University of Zurich, he had measured an energy source in the cerebral cortex which he felt might well be the human soul; unfortunately, his experiments with living subjects had resulted in the electrocution of a young man. That was followed by an embarrassing inquiry, a mysterious falling-out with Dr. Gruber, and, eventually, Hill's resignation from the faculty. But his research made good press and loosened purse strings, so young Miskatonic snapped him up. Cain found him cold and self absorbed, but his patients tended to live. In his mind, that more than outweighed his many personal failings.

Cain lingered by the door, watching Hill's technique. His hands seemed to become a part of whatever instrument they held, whether wielding a scalpel or, as now, deftly maneuvering the laser to pick small tendrils of flesh from the opening.

Handing Scott the pen-shaped implement, Hill picked up a long wooden Q-tip and inserted it into the hole.

"Lesions in the brain tissue and reported epilepti-form convulsions lead us to suspect cysticercosis," he said in a deep, resonant voice. His assistant brought over a test tube, into which Hill placed the Q-tip. "Mark that one for *Taenia solium*, whose presence will confirm the hypothesis. I'll want another for red corpuscles and a third for possible traces of calcification." He stole a look at his watch. "Note, too, that we were in and out in three minutes. A fraction of the time a scalpel would have required." Cain shook his head. Hill had an uncanny sense about the brain which transcended what could be learned from books and classes. He was an artist in the truest sense of the word, a man using mind and instinct to mold the medium in which he was working.

A hand clapped down on Cain's shoulder. Spinning, he saw the old but still cherubic face of Dean Halsey, his wide smile splitting his rosy cheeks.

"I'm sorry, Dan, I didn't mean to scare you. We arrived while you were in the other room."

The intern shrugged. "It wasn't too bad. I just didn't know anybody was here."

A nasal voice from behind the dean said, "You mean... anybody *else*."

Cain peered into the shadows as a small young man stepped forward. Wearing a pencil-thin black tie, black suit, and a pair of black-framed glasses, he looked every inch an undertaker. But there was something in his manner that made him different, something snide in the thin, unsmiling mouth, something arrogant, not servile, in the rigid posture.

Dean Halsey chuckled. "Herbert, Daniel Cain may not be much of a linguist, but he *is* one of Miskatonic's best young hopes for the future of medicine. He may be soft-spoken" - he clapped Cain again on the shoulder - "but he's as determined as they come in the emergency room." He motioned the other man over. "Dan, this is Herbert West. He's also rather the quiet type. He'll be joining you in your third year. Herbert was doing independent research in Switzerland with Dr. Gruber shortly before he died. I'm sure you two will work very well together."

West was not looking at Cain but past him, at Dr. Hill, who was just finishing up with the autopsy.

Cain extended his hand. "Pleased to meet you. What were you researching?"

West brushed past the outstretched hand and walked closer toward Hill. "Death," he said tersely, watching as the neurosurgeon pulled off his mask. West stared ahead intently, burning that first full view of Hill's face into his memory. He wanted it clear and vivid, accessible when he needed a spur in the dark solitude of his laboratory.

Looking toward them, Hill smiled broadly when he spotted Dean Halsey. He came forward quickly, with long-legged strides.

"Allan! So good of you to stop by!"

"Good to be here!" Halsey answered in his raspy voice.

"My word, we don't see *nearly* enough of you around here since they moved you to the front office. How've you been? And how was Israel?"

"To tell the truth, I'm in slightly better shape than the Middle East. The security there is absolute hell. It took hours just to get into and out of the airport. But we'll have to have dinner soon; there were some excellent papers presented at Technion."

Halsey missed Cain's little smile. He and Megan had also enjoyed her father's two-week trip enormously. Her new project was to get him to go to the convention of deans at UCLA over Labor Day.

"Well." Halsey rubbed his hands together. "I was just giving our newest student, Herbert West here, the not-so-grand tour. This should interest you, Carl: he worked with Hans Gruber."

"Oh?" Hill's smile wavered somewhat, and his eyelids drooped suspiciously. "That's quite a switch, Zurich to Arkham."

"The greater adjustment will be the loss of a dear friend and respected colleague."

"Yes, of course. I was very sorry to hear of his passing. However, I'm sure he is well represented by his successor."

If West were flattered, his face failed to reflect it. He continued to stare at Hill, something unpleasant burning in the back of his eyes.

"Mr. West," Halsey resumed in his ebullient tones, "allow me to formally present our eminent brain researcher and grant machine, Dr. Carl Hill."

"I know your work, Dr. Hill. Quite well, in fact. Your theory on the location of the will in the brain is" - he smiled suddenly, wickedly - "very interesting."

Hill thanked him with a nod, but his eyes never left the student.

"It's interesting, Doctor, though derivative of Dr. Gruber's research in the early seventies. So derivative, in fact, that in Europe it's actually considered plagiary."

The comment turned Halsey around, a shocked look on his soft features. Hill said nothing, merely stared; Cain was surprised but intrigued by the brash young newcomer.

"Furthermore, I would point out that your support of the twelve-minute limit on the life of the brainstem after death is in error-"

"*Six* to twelve minutes, Mr..."

"West. Herbert West. Frankly, Doctor, what I'm saying is that your work on brain death is... outdated."

A pair of veins bulged prominently on either side of Hill's high forehead, and his chin rose defiantly. Though Halsey was still stunned, he stepped casually between them, his back to West.

"Uh... Carl, while I'm thinking of it, we're having a Grant Committee meeting on Thursday. Why don't you come for dinner then? Megan and I would both enjoy it."

The neurosurgeon smiled stiffly. "Why, I'd love to, Allan. I look forward to it." His gaze rolled back to West. "And I'm looking forward to seeing you in class, Mr. West. I'm looking forward to that *very* much."

Hill stalked away, followed by West's angry gaze; Halsey glanced at his watch.

"Dan, I've just remembered a call I have to make. If you've got a minute, would you mind showing Mr. West the emergency room?"

"No problem. I was heading there myself."

Thanking him, Halsey followed Hill from the autopsy room. When they were alone, Cain took a deep breath.

"Nice going. You certainly know how to impress the right people."

The young man gazed at the double doors. His features were relaxed now, almost pleasant as he looked up at Cain.

"Were you referring to Dean Halsey or Dr. Hill?"

"Actually, the Dean didn't look too thrilled

with you, but I was talking about Mr....I mean Dr. Hill. He can be a son of a bitch, but he has a lot of influence here. I assume you're taking his class."

West sneered. "I'll be sitting in the classroom, yes."

"Well, if I were you, I'd sit without the chip on my shoulder. An F from him is like a bad review in the *New York Times*. It's tough to stay in business after that."

"Oh, I think I'll be around all right."

The sneer brightened into a smile, a cherishing of something unspoken. Cain did a poor job of concealing his displeasure.

"*As* for the rest of the tour, Mr. Cain, you needn't bother. If you'll just direct me to the microscopy lab-"

"The lab?"

"Yes, I'd like to take a look at the equipment. Is there something wrong with that?"

"No, it's just that... Are you sure? Halsey may not have told you, but this place was laid out by a gal who designs mouse mazes for a living. It was someone's idea of a great way to get publicity."

West regarded Cain. "Am I sure, Daniel? Yes, I'm sure. I'm always sure."

Cain was annoyed, the more so when West's head cocked to one side - like Rufus - it struck him, when the cat lay on the opposite side of the kitchen, watching to see whether what was being dumped into his bowl was worth getting up for. Cain felt like handing the diminutive West his round little head.

"Tell me something, though, Mr. Cain... Daniel. If the Dean thinks so highly of you, why are you on morgue detail?"

West's interest caught Cain off-guard. "We lost someone we shouldn't have. I guess I was pretty upset."

"Was it the hospital's fault?"

"No, we did all we could. We just keep missing, that's all, and this time it got to me. So they sent me here for some R & R." Encouraged by West's openness, Cain decided to give him another chance. "I hear you were there when Professor Gruber died. That must have been rough."

West shrugged. "Mostly on him."

Cain's displeasure returned, etched in the deep lines of a frown. West seemed not to notice. He looked at his watch.

"Now then, the microscopy lab?"

Cain gave up trying to be the man from Welcome Wagon. He provided directions in a perfunctory fashion, and West left without a "thank you" or a "nice to have met you," just a nod and a swift departure. Cain watched him go. Herbert West had to be one of the most unpleasant people he'd ever met. Although there was a refreshing courtliness and professionalism about him, he was too astringent to be admired. If he lasted a week at Miskatonic, Cain would be very, very surprised.

Noticing that Scott was still cleaning up, Cain offered to deliver the specimens. Scott seemed grateful, almost shocked to have someone pay him notice. The men chatted a bit about the laser drill and about the New England Patriots, though it surprised Cain that Scott seemed happier and more animated when the conversation turned to football. When Scott first came to the school, the drill was all he talked about. As he walked toward the downstairs lab, Cain suddenly found himself in an upbeat mood. Part of it was being able to see Megan after having put in a two-day stretch at the hospital. But part of it was also, he realized - and without guilt - that he was looking forward to Hill's class the following morning. He always enjoyed the lectures and demonstrations, but Cain suspected that this class would be special. He even wondered if he should call his old physics professor, Dr. St. Mary. He had a feeling that a rare phenomenon was about to occur, the head-on collision of the irresistible force and the immovable object.

Chapter 3

APARTMENT TO SHARE!
3rd-year medical student needs roommate
Must be quiet & keep regular hours
Must like cats
Contact: Dan Cain
666 Darkmore
555-8785

Cain tacked the note to the bulletin board in the well-traveled corridor of Derleth Hall, then stood back. There were at least twenty requests for roommates, most with the rent listed and bragging about what a bargain the place was; he hoped that his more austere approach would attract a higher grade of person.

"Hell, right now I'll be happy if it attracts *anyone.*"

It had been tough since Eddie Grimley had dropped out. His father had money, and Eddie had spent it lavishly on them both. But Eddie finally faced the fact that what he wanted to be was a dancer and not a doctor, so he dropped out, leaving Cain with a gabled six-room house on Hawthorne Street - and a thousand-dollar-a-month nut to crack all by himself.

Casting a furtive look around, Cain pulled down a few of the more desirable notices and dropped them in the trash. Feeling canny if not virtuous, he turned to find Megan wagging a scolding finger at him.

"Not nice, Mr. Ex-Boy Scout."

Cain flushed. "Megan! Where'd you come from?"

"Been following you, badness." She put the back of her hand to her brow and threw her head back. "God, Dan, where will it all end? Getting rid of the competition today, trading insider information tomorrow. Pretty soon I'll be baking hacksaws into pound cakes."

"Megan, I need the dough."

The young woman scowled. "Hey, sourpuss, I was only kidding! I'm *glad* to see you do a little scheming for once. Next, maybe you'll even tell the Wicked Witch of the West to go screw herself!"

"C'mon, Megan. Dr. Harrod is a dedicated physician-"

"She's a hard biddy who hates my father and runs her interns into the ground."

Cain laid Megan's books on the radiator and pulled her to him. "She has no choice, and, besides, some of us have the stamina of bulls."

"Yeah, Joe Hunk, I've heard that about you."

"What do you mean?"

"I mean, after she heard we were serious, your ex-pal Loree took me aside and told me about how you broke her heart and about your flings with what were their names? Jan and Elizabeth and Isobel. And I even remember the time you did with no less a personage than Miss Poland herself, Paula Olszewski."

"Loree was jealous, and those other girls meant nothing. They lasted a week each when I first came here."

"You were just being studly, huh?"

"No, I just hadn't dated in *years*, and they were a novelty. If it makes you happy, I'll admit my head was way up my gastrointestinal tract-"

"What d'you mean 'was,' big boy?"

He kissed her forehead. "I'll overlook that, Meg, because for the last six months the only woman I've cared about has blond hair" - he ran his hands through her long blond hair - "big blue eyes" - he kissed her above each eye - "a precious ski nose…"

"Precious? I think I'm gonna puke!"

" - and perfectly formed red lips..." He kissed her lightly on the mouth and stayed there.

After a long moment, Megan pulled away, giggling nervously. "Watch it, bub."

"You still sick? Try Tigan."

"No, I mean I *am* the Dean's daughter."

"So?"

"I've got a reputation to protect."

Cain snickered. "I thought you liked it when I was aggressive."

"I do, but not in the hallway when class is about to let out."

"As if anyone cares."

"Wake up and smell the coffee, Dan. There're about twenty-odd professors who'd love to embar-rass Daddy as a way of thanking him for budget cuts."

"That's his problem, not mine. Either you get Conan the Barbarian or Grandpa Amos McCoy."

Megan grinned. "That's what I love about you, Dan. All the gray areas. Tell you what. I'll take Walter Brennan in the classroom, Arnold Schwarze-negger in the bedroom."

"That wasn't an option, so *I* get to pick!" Cain's eyes opened hungrily, and he kissed her again. Megan struggled playfully. "Surrender, woman, my ardor

43

knows no bounds."

"Dan, no!"

"No? There's always Paula-"

"No, I mean not here!"

He kissed her neck. "How about there?"

"Dan, no... Not *here!*"

"Dan, yes! ..Yes, *there!*"

Perspiration ran down Cain's back and mingled with Megan's as they thrashed rhythmically on the bed. It stung when it dribbled into the scratches Megan had given him, but Cain didn't mind. This time around - their second in a row - he didn't have to distract himself by thinking of dinosaurs or Smurfs. His only thoughts were of Megan, and he loved every moment of it. After days of numbing wakefulness, of crisis upon crisis and people he couldn't help, time suddenly, blissfully no longer existed. Their bed was the whole world, and the entire population was Megan and him...

They slept afterwards, and then, as the setting sun shone over the roofs of the eighteenth-century homes and through the bedroom window, they woke and made love again.

Feet padded silently through the living room and down the corridor. The dark figure stopped, listened, entered the room, crept along stealthily. His eyes missed nothing as he navigated around the mounds of books and clothing. He climbed onto the dresser, crouched beneath the *Gray's Anatomy* poster, waited until the figures were still. Then, his legs tensed, he leaped onto Cain's back.

"Rufus! Hey, what is it, buddy?"

Cain flipped over, and the cat fled across the room, satisfied with his guerrilla exercise. Megan laughed.

"Did he scratch you?"

Cain felt the middle of his back. "Who can tell? It's like a battle zone back there."

The young woman playfully raked his chest. "If you can't stand the heat, don't light a fire." She looked at her Swatch and swung from the bed. "It's late. I have to go."

"No you don't. Stay."

The young woman began collecting her clothing which was strewn about the floor. "I can't. Daddy knows I'm here." She bent down, looked under the bed. "Dan, do you see my panties?"

Cain plucked the garment from the top of the lampshade, tossed them over.

"I don't care what your father knows. I really want you to stay the night."

"So do I, but we have to be reasonable! If I don't come home one night, just one night-"

"What will he do? Expel me?"

"He might very well. I'm sure he could think of a million other uses for that loan money."

"Yeah, like throwing another fancy dinner party for the rich and famous or going to some bullshit convention overseas."

"You're not being fair," Megan said, an edge in her voice. She slipped on the underpants, snuggled into her jeans. "Daddy's doing an excellent job."

"The word is *number*, Meg. He's doing an excellent number... on you."

"Dan, I'm his only child, his baby-"

"Oh yeah?" Cain watched her pull on her bra. "When was the last time he took a good look at you?"

"I can tell you *exactly* when," she replied. "Nine years ago, when Mom left. To him I'm still in elementary school."

Cain shook his head. "That's real healthy for

both of you. Does he know he's way out of touch with the times?"

"No, and he doesn't care. That's just the way he is, the world's last living Puritan."

Cain huffed and folded his arms. "Well, I really hate it. You're his little girl, his hostess, his spy-"

"Only on the untenured."

"But you're also *my* fiancée. And that doesn't seem to matter as much as the rest of the crap."

Megan pulled on her shirt and cuddled up beside him. "Dan, the day you graduate, the *minute* you get your M.D., I'll marry you. Until then, I'll help you, and I'll be with you as much as I can. I promise."

"Which brings up another point. Not only won't you stay the night or move in, but you won't even *marry* me until I graduate. 'Cause if something happened and I had to drop out, Daddy wouldn't be able to say, 'My son-in-law, the doctor.' He'd be a leper to the trustees and to the good-old-boys network."

"That isn't it, and you know it," Megan chided. "Marriage is a full-time job, and right now you haven't got the time *or* the energy for it."

Cain threw up his arms. "Which brings us back to square one."

"Which isn't so bad," she laughed. "At least it gives me another ten months to housebreak you."

"Housebroken, is it?" Cain pulled the Star Trek sheet over his head, ghostlike, and began slowly to rise. "I'm going to have to teach you a lesson, my girl."

"Dan, what are you doing?" Smiling, Megan scooped up her books and backed away. So did Rufus, who scooted down to the cellar.

Dan said in a haunted whisper, "Hello, my pretty! You haven't been loved fully until you've made love to the dead..."

"Dan, stop!"

"You're not going to leave..."

"Dan, I don't *like* that!" Sidling from the bedroom to the living room, Megan swatted playfully at Cain's outstretched arms with a slim volume of Tennyson. "Dan, you're scaring me!"

"Then come to me, Megan Halsey. Come to me or suffer the consequences!"

"You'll suffer," she warned. "I'll kick you right in the balls!"

"The balls? The dead don't *have* balls!"

"Then I'll have you arrested."

"Balderdash! There's not a jury in the world that would convict me."

"Stop!"

"Not me, the infamous Doctor Dan, executed for lobotomizing a stuffy old college dean!"

Backing up against the front door, Megan felt for the knob. *"Stop!"*

"Why?" Cain chortled. "I've got you now! There's nowhere left to run, no one to hear your screams!"

Stealing a quick backward glance, Megan ducked under his grasping arms and pulled open the door. Turning, she ran smack into a small man in a black overcoat; standing stiffly on the stoop, he watched, bemused, as Megan shrieked and stumbled back into the house.

"Megan?" Cain fumbled with the sheet. "What is it? What'd I miss?" He managed to extricate his face from the folds and stared with surprise at the visitor. "West!"

"Hello, Mr. Cain."

Cain quickly knotted the sheet around his waist. "Uh... hi. Can we help you?"

West drew Cain's notice from his shirt pocket,

held it up.

"Oh, you're here about the apartment." Cain glanced uneasily from West to Megan and back to the bedroom. "Say, would you excuse me just *one* second? It's... cold."

Cain scooted off. Megan watched him go, then turned back to West. "Won't you come in?"

"Thank you."

West smiled tightly and stepped inside, his eyes on the young woman. She hugged her books to her chest.

"I startled you," he offered unapologetically.

"Yes, you did."

"This street... is rather isolated. I don't imagine you get many uninvited visitors."

"I... I wouldn't know. I'm not here that often."

"Of course."

Cain came rushing back, buttoning his shirt. "Sorry about that," he gushed. "Doctors can't afford to get sick. Bad for their credibility." He took Megan's hand. "So, Herbert West, may I introduce my fiancée, Megan Halsey."

West bowed slightly. "Miss Halsey."

"Mr. West."

"And are you also studying medicine?"

She rocked her head from side to side. "Informally. I enjoy it, but I don't want to practice it."

Cain swept his hand behind him. "I'm afraid the place is still kind of a mess, Mr. West."

West's gaze shifted from Megan to the living room cluttered with an old sofa, an ironing board, two armchairs, books stacked on the floor, and a compact disc setup.

"Call me Herbert," he said, walking into the living room and taking in his surroundings. "And it's quite all right about the room. Our instruments must be antiseptic, but not our homes. I like to be surrounded by... life."

His hosts exchanged puzzled glances; spotting the corridor, West headed for it.

"So," Megan said, following him with Cain in tow, "my father tells me you've just come from Europe. Where exactly?"

"Switzerland. Zurich."

"Lovely city."

"I didn't get to see much of the city. My work was extremely time-consuming."

"That's a shame," she said, casting a dark look at Cain.

Cain shrugged. Megan was sizing West up and not liking what she found. Cain gave her a disapproving poke in the back. She ignored him and pressed on. "And what was Dr. Gruber like? Daddy says he was pretty famous."

"Yes. He's 'pretty' famous."

Cain thought he detected mockery in West's voice. From her unhappy expression, Megan detected more and liked it even less.

West stopped. "Tell me, Daniel, does this building have a basement?"

"Sure does."

"Dry?"

"Like a desert. They built 'em better a hundred and fifty years ago."

West nodded approvingly. "Where is it? I'd like to see it."

"Door to your left. Just watch the steps, though. They're rotting, and I'm not insured."

West pulled the heavy door open, and the trio descended the rickety wooden stairs. When Cain tugged the light cord, West's eyes went wide.

"Oh, yes... yes, Daniel!"

"Nice, huh?"

"Nice? It's perfection."

Megan put her arms around Cain's waist. "I think it's spooky. The owner died down here... he wasn't found for weeks."

"What a waste," said West.

Cain and Megan watched with a blend of confusion and distaste as West moved through the dusty old chairs and cartons shut with peeling tape. He looked up at the four transom windows, all of which were bricked up, and nodded approvingly; he bent to examine an electrical outlet and smiled broadly.

"This is simply perfect."

Cain thought of the bills piled high on the kitchen table and put his doubts aside. "It's a great room," he agreed. "I'd always meant to put a pool table down here, with a big Tiffany lamp, but I could never put together the dough."

"A Tiffany lamp? Come now, Daniel, don't be so plebeian."

Cain chewed the inside of his cheek. From silly in the morning to plebeian at night. At least he was coming up in the world; by the following day he might actually be upgraded to a mere fool. Megan squeezed him tightly, and he looked down. She was very cross.

Cain wormed from her arms. "So, what would *you* do with the place, Herbert?"

West peeked under a tarpaulin, examined the small refrigerator underneath. "Make it a laboratory, of course. I'll pay extra, don't worry-"

Megan frowned. "Mr. West, aren't you getting ahead of yourself?"

"In what way?"

"Well, you'll want to look at other places, do some comparison shopping."

"Rooms in Arkham are at a premium. Indeed,

I'm curious. How *did* you ever find such a place, Daniel?"

"I was real lucky," Cain admitted. "The man who owned it died suddenly - a strange guy, a horror writer named Phillips. In fact, he worked down here, even had the windows bricked up for atmosphere. Anyway, when he passed away, the family in California didn't want anything to do with it. They let me take a four-year lease just as long as I promised not to touch the old man's junk."

"Is there an attic?"

"It's small but empty."

"Excellent. Then we can move these things up there." He stopped his examination and looked expectantly at Cain. "I think this will be just fine. I have my things outside. Shall I move in now?"

Megan stepped suddenly between them, facing Cain. "Uh... look, I have to go, Dan. I think you and Mr. West have a *lot* to discuss before you decide anything."

Her eyes said it all: she didn't want West around. Cain sympathized; he had been hoping for someone a little less austere. He looked over at his classmate, who had already reached into his pocket and withdrawn his wallet.

"Herbert, Meg is right. Don't you think we should talk about this?"

"Why, Daniel? I've already decided." West pulled out several bills. "What are you paying here?"

"Eight hundred. Utilities included."

West removed ten one-hundred-dollar bills. "Here's my share, first and last month. I'll be paying five hundred since I'll require the downstairs and the attic."

Cain stared at the proffered money; Megan tugged the front of his shirt.

"Dan - can I talk to you?"

"You know," West assured them, "you'll never even know I'm here." He paused, said pointedly, "Except, of course, on the first of the month. Dr. Gruber left me quite a bit of his estate. In fact, if you ever need more, just ask. Money holds no particular fascination for me."

The young woman turned. "Mr. West, may I ask you something?"

"Anything you like, Miss Halsey."

"You didn't say *why* you left Switzerland."

He smiled benignly. "There was no more I could learn there, naturally." He looked over at Cain. "Do we have a deal?"

The young man looked down at his feet. After a moment, he reached out suddenly and accepted the money. "Done."

"Done!" West smiled, then took off for the steps. "I'll get my things!"

"Need any help?" Cain shouted.

West didn't answer, and, when she heard him scuttle out the front door, Megan slammed her books onto an old upright piano, sending clouds of dust in every direction.

"Tell me, Daniel Jonathan Cain, was I being a little too subtle?"

"What do you mean?"

"Did you miss the fact that I think the guy is a total creep?"

Cain pocketed the money. "Guess what, hon? I don't like him much either, but his money's the right denomination, and what does it matter who takes the room? If it isn't going to be you, it might just as well be Larry Tolbot."

"Who?"

"The Wolfman. All it means is that you'll have

52

to be a little quieter when we make love."

She tapped her toe angrily. "*If* we make love, you mean."

Cain picked up her books and headed for the stairs. "If that's a declaration of war, I'm sure I can always ally myself with Miss Poland."

"Be my guest."

"I'll tell Professor Norvig you're spying on him."

"I don't care."

"I'll tell your dad you slept here while he was in Israel."

Megan spun. "You wouldn't."

He smiled. "You're right. I'd much rather do it than reminisce about it."

Cain held out his hand, and, sighing, the young woman took it. "Okay, have yourself your odd little roomie. Just don't expect me to have much to do with him. He's obnoxious and he's short."

"Frankly, my dear, I get the feeling Herbert West would just as soon you, me, and the rest of the world leave him alone. Which is exactly what I intend to do."

So saying, Cain walked his fiancée to her car, while, grinning broadly despite his huffing and grunting, West dragged his trunks and suitcases from the rented station wagon along the curving concrete walk.

Dr. Carl Hill sat sipping scotch in his apartment, lying back on the recliner and staring out at the river. Only minutes before, he'd canceled Babette, the girl from Boston he'd reserved for the evening. The appearance of Gruber's former associate made it impossible for him to think of anything but why the youth had really come to Miskatonic - and if whatever had happened to the professor could possibly happen to him as well.

"Not unless the boy is using voodoo," he told himself without quite believing it.

He put the glass to his lips, realized there were many ways to poison someone, and reluctantly put the glass aside. He folded his hands on his belly. Sighing away his fears, he retrieved the glass.

"Life is full of danger," he decided. "Death is all around us."

The loft, for example, had once been death - an Ogan Chemical processing plant which had been closed down when the river turned red and all the fish died. Kenneth Ogan had taken the spillage seriously enough to leave his San Clemente estate and fly east to personally lock the door.

"Now they're busy burying the stuff in the Appalachian Mountains," Hill mumbled, feeling the effects of the drink and the two Valium he'd washed down. "You can't live in fear of dying, or you can't live at all!" He saluted the bottle of Valium. "Without chemicals, life itself would be impossible!"

Still, West's presence troubled him. After their meeting, he'd borrowed the youth's file from Dean Halsey. In it, West had outlined, very amorphously, studies of the brain he hoped to accomplish. That was why Halsey had taken pains to introduce them. West had an ambitious program to study the rage center of the brain and find a way to subjugate it without lobotomy. That sounded laudable enough on the surface, but nothing in his file from Switzerland hinted at any similar work. Most of his classes were in chemistry, not the brain.

Halsey, of course, hadn't bothered to make that analysis. All he saw was the last student of a brilliant scientist asking to enroll in his institution.

"What does research matter when prestige can be had?"

It was amazing, he reflected, that so shallow and plain a man as Halsey could have created such a radiant creature as Megan. He looked over at the thick file he'd brought home, the file he'd expected to go through slowly, lovingly, before Babette arrived tonight. The photographs, the notes, the mementoes - He got up and refilled his glass.

"No sense getting aroused now," he cautioned himself, and put the file back in his briefcase. He sat back down, and his mind returned to Herbert West. The youth was obviously a hothead and would tip his hand soon enough. What he had to do was encourage that, not let the boy bait him as he had today, force him to lose his temper. He must retain the upper hand.

West was only twenty-four, half his age. He'd seen nothing of the world and even less, he was sure, of medicine. The surgeon fell asleep in the recliner, relishing all the ways he could use his position to draw and quarter the brash young man...

Chapter 4

The students watched attentively as Scott wheeled the table into the classroom. On it was a young woman, whom Cain recognized as Wendy Grant. Her parents had wanted her body donated to science, and Hill had wasted little time claiming it; he wanted a fresh brain for this morning's class. As usual, what Hill wanted Dean Halsey was only too happy to give.

Cain noticed that the incision in her torso where the autopsy had been performed was only perfunctorily repaired, and for the first time in his brief career he felt an unpleasant sense of ghoulishness. Since she had been entrusted to them, ailing, to her final appearance here in Hill's class, the poor young woman had been nothing more than a slab of meat. Scott situated the table so that the very top of the woman's head overlapped the sink. Thanking his assistant, Dr. Hill rose from his desk and stood behind the body. He was wearing rubber gloves, a green smock and cap, and a white apron; his manner was casual as he picked up a scalpel in one hand and, after examining it, bent over the dead girl and put the other hand beneath her head. Lifting it slightly, be made a slow lateral cut, speaking while he did.

"You make the incision at the base of the skull,

cutting away enough of the fascia to get your fingers in."

He lay the scalpel on the tray and snaked his fingers beneath the flap of skin.

"Then, grasping firmly with both hands, you pull the skin forward, over the skull."

There was a slurping sound as flesh separated from bone, clots of blood plopping and oozing into the sink.

"It's very much like peeling a large orange," Hill said, glancing briefly into the classroom, a half-smile playing about his lips. The quip defused some of the queasy tension that had settled on the room, although one student, a proctologist who was taking the course to meet a minimum requirement, had to turn away to keep from vomiting.

Hill quickly regained his serious demeanor. "Once the skull is plainly visible, you take the bone saw and cut around the perimeter."

As Hill did just that, Cain marveled again at his hands. Hill held the instrument firmly but delicately as the fanlike blades threw bone dust into the air. His dexterity and attentiveness must make him quite a doting lover, Cain couldn't help but reflect.

When Hill finished, he laid the saw aside and, with a hand on either side of the skull, gently tugged off its top. He set it on the instrument tray and picked up a pair of scissors, carefully snipping away sinew inside the brain-case. This done, he gently inserted his fingers and withdrew the contents. He stood erect, cradling the brain in his hands.

"There you have it, ladies and gentlemen: the human brain. Once the brainstem of an individual-I'm talking about the reticular activating system, heart regulation respiratory system-once these activities cease, the brain can only survive an additional six to twelve minutes."

His eyes came to sit on Herbert West, who was seated in the front row.

"I repeat: six to twelve minutes."

West looked away with mild disgust and began drumming the eraser of his pencil on the desk. Hill ignored him.

"Brain death is true death, at least for those of us who don't believe in religious dogma. Brain death brings about an irreversible conclusion to life, a-"

West snapped his pencil in two and let both halves fall to the floor. The silence grew heavy as Hill glowered at him. West met his gaze, making a point of picking up another pencil and holding it tightly between both fists.

The surgeon briefly considered giving West the floor. He would let him rave so that the others would see how unbalanced he was, and it would put an end to his little disruptions. But Gruber had been too sharp a judge of talent to ally himself with a fool; if West's intent were to get under his skin, he would find another way of doing it. Against the instincts crying out inside, Hill ignored the challenge by turning and laying the brain on the instrument tray. "We all want to retain our personalities in some idyllic afterlife," Hill went on evenly. "We all pray for some miracle, some drug, potion, pill. Perhaps, though, it takes something more than that, something *internal*. We achieve our goals in life by being obsessed with them. Perhaps it takes that same kind of desire to transcend death-a supreme effort, an incredible surge of will, to keep alive and as a unified whole the electricity of the brain, what we colloquially call the soul. I believe this is true; I believe it is the only means by which humans can become immortal."

West broke a second pencil, and Hill snapped

stiffly to attention. Cain looked from the surgeon to West. He felt his own pulse race; he could imagine what Hill was going through.

The lanky man stared out through hooded eyes. "Is there a problem, *Mr.* West?"

"There is indeed, *Dr.* Hill."

"One that cannot wait until after class?"

West's upper lip curled with disdain. "Class? This isn't a class, it's nothing more than a primer on the dark ages of medicine. Come into the twentieth century!"

The doctor's patience evaporated. His forehead reddened, the veins pulsing; his arms hung straight down, the fists like rock. "I think we've heard quite enough from you, my impudent young *colleague.*"

"I'd rather be impudent than ignorant."

"In my judgment, you are both!"

West replied slowly, "In that case, your judgment is faulty... like your theories."

Hill grabbed a beaker and was a moment away from throwing it when he saw the disbelieving looks on the faces of his students. Looking out at them, he realized that 'he' had lost this round, that West had made *him* look unbalanced. There was nothing to do now but retreat and regroup.

Clearing his throat, he set the beaker back on the counter and took a moment to collect himself. "The fact is, Mr. West, what you think is not important. Whether *you* like it or not, it is you who must please *me*, and not vice versa. Therefore, I strongly suggest that you leave here and acquire a much-improved *attitude.*" He noticed the litter around West's chair and said snidely, "And while you're at it, I also suggest you get yourself a pen. Both will be necessary before I allow you to return here tomorrow." He turned back to the counter, saying over his shoulder, "That will be all for

60

today. Class dismissed."

West jumped up. "No, Doctor, it is *you* who should be dismissed!"

Hill felt his control slipping again. He came around slowly. "What did you say?"

"Isn't it bad enough you left Switzerland in disgrace? Must you compound your sins by standing up there and teaching such… drivel? These people are here to learn, and you're closing their minds before they even have a chance!"

Hill tugged off his gloves. "And what are *you* here for, Mr. West? Certainly not to learn!"

"There *is* nothing I can learn from you! In fact, you should have stolen *more* of Gruber's ideas. Then at least you'd *have* ideas!"

From the corner of his eye, Hill saw that the class was filling out much too slowly. They were hanging on every word, which only added to his displeasure. Throwing his apron aside, he strode to West's side. Although he towered over the diminutive youth, West stood his ground defiantly.

"Whether it's merely a misconception under which you labor, or whether you suffer from complete dementia, I promise you this: it is going to be a singular pleasure to fail you!"

Hill turned and stalked from the classroom, the other students shaking their heads as they followed. Their manner belied their sympathies, whispered conversation and uneasy backward glances charging West with crimes ranging from disrespect to lunacy. West ignored them and also Cain, who was the last to leave. He'd been hovering by the door, deciding whether to have a long chat with his roommate or back off. He finally opted for the latter, seeing only hostility in West's small eyes.

When everyone was gone, West parted his lips

61

slightly. He'd been sucking air through his nose, which caused his nostrils to flare and gave him a bat-like look. He took a calming breath.

"We shall see," he uttered coldly, "just who will fail, you silly little man."

Collecting his books, West noticed the brain in the tray and went to it. After casting a furtive glance toward the corridor, the young man casually tore a fistful of paper towels from a roll and wrapped the organ inside, slipping it into the folds of his overcoat. A quick check of the toe tag revealed what Cain had mentioned earlier, as they had moved some of the larger pieces of furniture from the basement to the attic: this was the girl who had died of a heart attack the day before. A cruel smile played about his lips as he headed for the corridor, the hem of his coat -trailing an occasional drop of blood.

We shall see, Carl Hill, he thought exultantly. *You, Miss Grant, and I… shall see!*

Chopin peppered the air; the music, the wine, and the events of the day lulled Dean Halsey into a state of relaxed satisfaction. Seated beneath the crystal chandelier of his spacious dining room, he leaned to his side and thanked his daughter for an excellent meal, then regarded Dr. Hill.

"An excellent meal for a scientist who excels." He raised his nearly empty wineglass. "A half-million dollars, Carl, and not in small monthly doses. Half now, half when you or any member of your team publishes the particulars about the drill."

Hill smiled, but his mind was not on the grant. Having the money to refine the drill and build more than their one prototype was important, but Scott and the others could do most of the programming and engineering. The technology itself was merely a sideline to the main event, his continuing search for the

62

seat of the will and the soul.

Yet, at the moment, his mind was not on that either. Nor was it on Megan Halsey. Ordinarily, he could not keep his eyes from her. Whether the stately young woman was in a striking pants-suit, as now, or in a bathing suit as she swam at the university pool, or in tight shorts as she played tennis in the park, he savored the sight of her flesh and form, his mind swept up in how he would worship it and her, if given the chance.

The fingers of one hand worked lightly along the baroque handle of his steak knife. Though his eyes were on Megan Halsey's breasts, tonight he didn't see them. Nor were his ears attuned to the droning of Dean Halsey.

Tonight he was consumed with Herbert West. He couldn't fathom what West wanted from him.

Money? He didn't seem the type. Retribution? That made sense, but whom was he avenging?

He'd worked with Gruber, so that was the likely choice.

Hill considered the possibility. Much depended on how much West knew about what had gone on in Switzerland. The young man was aware that he'd worked with Gruber, that he'd used the late scientist's ideas as a springboard. But in his single-minded devotion to Gruber, did he know how much farther he'd gone with those ideas? Did West know of the computer program he and Scott had written to scan the human brain and ignore all electrical activity save that generated by the cerebral cortex? Was he aware of the surges he'd measured whenever the subjects were presented with a moral dilemma? Did he know that he'd spent years on his own expanding on Gruber's very simplistic notions?

Probably not. West wasn't the type to see gray

areas. His world was black and white.

He wondered, though, if West might also be here for Nancy.

West had to know about her dying when the program had shut down her brain instead of merely ignoring superfluous readings. Gruber or someone else at the school had to have mentioned it. But did he also know that the brain death of Nancy Joseph had not been the sole reason for his dismissal? That his problems did not stem from that or from literally having burned the student's brain inside her skull while he had hastily tried to write a program to reactivate it? That he was dismissed *not* for his experiments, for she'd signed all the appropriate releases, but because it was expressly against school policy for professors and students to be lovers?

Perhaps one of Nancy's relatives had gotten to him. Perhaps they'd seen, in West, an ideal means to strike back.

Perhaps.

Or maybe it was Willett who had sent West here. Although Hill had gone to Switzerland in 1978 with a title equal to Gruber's, it was understood that he was technically the elder scientist's assistant. That relationship had ended when Gruber petitioned Dr. Willett to prevent Hill from conducting research on humans. Willett delighted in playing scientists against one another in an endless quest for greater productivity and more Nobel winners, and saw the friction as healthy. That philosophy dissipated when Nancy died. He was sent packing. Gruber was given all the power. The trustees had demanded both and normalcy was restored.

Now that Gruber was gone, Willett had no one to collect honors… or grants. He might very well have encouraged West to seek him out.

Hill considered it all, then asked himself if it mattered. Short of satisfying his curiosity, would the knowledge help to forestall another confrontation? Would it leave him calm enough so that West's taunts would roll off his back?

"Planning to operate on my Drexel, Carl?"

The scientist looked up. Dean Halsey was smiling stupidly, pointing toward his plate. Hill glanced down. The knife handle was gripped tightly in his fist, the tip of the blade pressed to the tablecloth. Chuckling uncomfortably, Hill lay the knife aside.

"Sorry, Allan. Unwillingness to see the meal ended, you know."

Halsey laughed. "I understand. My daughter *is* a superb cook."

Hill held her bright eyes with his. "She is indeed... superb."

Megan shifted uneasily in her seat as her father lifted his glass.

"Before the others arrive for the meeting - and I know how this sort of thing embarrasses you, Carl, but, dammit, you're going to sit through it - I would like to propose a toast: to the National Science Foundation, for recognizing the genius of Dr. Carl Hill and for awarding the Miskatonic Medical School its largest grant *ever*. Carl, your new laser drill is going to revolutionize neurosurgery."

Megan looked down, and Hill's eyes rolled from hers to those of her father.

"To the Foundation. And to Miskatonic."

The men drank deeply, but Megan took only a sip, then played absently with the stem of her glass. Her father smiled benignly.

"That's all right, sweetheart, you can drink up. We're celebrating."

"I know, Daddy, but I have to go soon."

65

Hill's brows arched sympathetically. "After preparing such a feast? You must be tired."

"Of course she is. You know, Carl, my baby didn't microwave a thing. Everything came out of the oven."

"And tasted it." Hill dipped his glass toward her.

"It was nothing, really. The stove did most of the work. Besides, I have a study date with Dan."

Hill's features clouded. "Dan? Daniel Cain?" Megan nodded, and Hill stared into his glass. "Herbert West has moved in with him, hasn't he?"

"For the time being. I - I'm not sure they're really going to be happy with each other."

"Are they too alike?"

The doorbell chimed, and Megan rose. "Hardly. I'm not even sure Mr. West has any interests outside his work."

"Precisely my point."

Megan stiffened and said sweetly, pointedly, "I assure you, Dr. Hill, Dan has an interest in other things. Now, if you'll excuse me, that must be him at the door."

After she'd gone, Hill peered thoughtfully at Halsey. "So... your daughter is seeing Cain. Do you think that's wise Allan?"

"What do you mean?"

"Oh, just that Cain is an ambitious young man without much money. I'd hate to think that he was seeing your daughter simply to try and use her to influence you."

"A moderm-day Pocahontas and Powhatan, eh? You know me better than that, Carl. All that matters to me is making Miskatonic the top medical school in the nation, and that means kowtowing to my professors, not my students."

The young couple entered then, and Halsey rose to shake the young man's hand.

"Good to see you relaxing, Dan!"

"It's only a short break, sir. We've both got some reading to do on spirochetal jaundice."

"Spirochetosis icterohaemorrhagica," Hill noted dryly.

Cain looked over. "Hello, Dr. Hill." They shook hands across the table. "I almost didn't recognize you without your smock and cap."

"Sort of like Superman without the cape," Dean Halsey noted. "Would you join us for a glass of wine?"

Cain checked with Megan, who counseled him with a barely perceptible shake of her head.

"Actually, we have some work to do. It'd be better if we got to it while we're still fresh."

"Why don't you study here?" Hill suggested. "You'll be fresher still."

"Thanks, but... Chopin puts me to sleep. I'll have her home soon, don't worry."

"Well then." Hill shot to his feet. "May I offer one last toast?"

"By all means."

Hill raised his glass. "To Megan - my esteemed colleague's capable, beautiful, loving daughter."

"Why, thank you," the Dean replied.

"Megan," Hill repeated solemnly, barely audibly, as he sat back down. "The obsession of *all* who fall under her spell."

The young woman acknowledged the toast with a small, stiff bow, then bent and kissed her father on the forehead. Pleasantly bidding the men a good evening, Cain followed her out.

Behind them, Hill was once again stroking the

knife.

Chapter 5

"He's a letch."

"You're being overly sensitive, Megan. Dr. Hill is a brilliant man."

Megan looked down into the book on her lap. "Fine, he's brilliant... he's a brilliant *letch*. I don't like being around him."

The living-room lights were turned off, save for the small Tiffany lamp beside the old sofa. Cain and Megan were seated beneath the lamp, reading from the same book.

"Forget Dr. Hill. Did you finish this stuff about Leptospira australis?"

"Screw it."

"Can't. They're wee itty-bitty things."

Megan shook her head, and, putting his arm around her, Cain nuzzled her on the cheek.

"Dan-"

He licked her jawline.

"Dan, please!"

Cain leaned back, throwing up his hands. "Okay, what is it?"

"I don't know." She bit her lower lip and said apologetically, "Look, it's not you. It's just a lot of little things."

"Like what?"

"Well-like West is always in his room with the door closed."

"So?"

"Do you ever see him? Does he ever eat?"

"Who *cares?*"

"*You* should! I mean, what do you really know about him?"

"Nothing except that he studied with Hans Gruber and pays for whatever he uses. He stuffed a buck in the toilet paper and two in the box of Meow Mix."

"In the cat food?"

"Yeah. Said he needed some protein for an experiment. Anyway, that kind of courtesy makes him okay in my book."

Megan squeezed Cain's hand. "Don't take this wrong, Dan, but you were raised by a spinster aunt who had the sensibilities of a nun. Your book of life experiences is slightly abridged."

"As opposed to you, whose life has been like a lending library."

"Sure, I've been around. The point is, I've got a sense about people that you don't. And I'm telling you that Dr. Hill is a pervert and Herbert West probably isn't much better."

Cain drummed on his knees. "So what? What if he *is* a little cracked?"

Megan studied his face. "All of this was bullshit, wasn't it?"

"What do you mean?"

"He bothers you too."

"Don't be ridiculous."

"He bothers you, and he bothers Rufus?"

"What?"

"Rufus is terrified of him. When West comes

in, he runs and hides."

Cain snickered. "Rufus runs and hides all the time. It's standard cat activity."

"Yes, but not when you and I are together! Then he's all over us, trying to get your attention." Megan paused, looked around. "Say, where is Rufus? I haven't seen him since we got here."

"It's okay. He's around here somewhere."

"Are you sure? I haven't heard him. Usually he at least knocks something over when I'm here." Rising urgently, Megan walked hunched about the room, whispering for the cat. "Here, Rufus. Here, kitty kitty."

Shaking his head, Cain stood and called more loudly, "Rufus! C'mon, you fat cat! Where are you, you mad animal?"

"Rufus? Heeeeere, Rufy."

"Hey, furball, don't you hide from me!"

Megan turned on another light and looked behind an armchair, then beneath it. Cain checked behind the drapes.

"Still think he's just hiding, Dan?"

"Of course. He's like Garfield, he could be anywhere."

"Fine. You take the kitchen, I'll check the bed-room."

Switching on the single bare bulb which lit the corridor, Megan proceeded slowly.

"Psssst. Rufus! You under the bed?"

On her way to the bedroom, Megan passed West's room and saw an eerie light seeping under the door. It was moving and fluorescent, with a slightly yellow cast. She rapped lightly on the door.

"Mr. West, are you in there? It's Megan." There was no answer, and after inquiring again, she tried the door. It was unlocked, and Megan opened it

71

slowly.

Even in the dim light, Megan could see that the walls were covered with charts and diagrams. Most of them showed the human brain, some the brains and vital organs of other animals, including cats.

The glow itself was coming from a small refrigerator which sat against the near wall, tucked between a cot and a large lab table, partly obscured by the latter. Walking slowly around it and peering across the countless rows of chemical powders and solutions, Megan saw that a vial standing in front of the bulb was causing the yellowish tint. She also saw why the refrigerator door was open. Something was in the way.

It was Rufus's tail.

Megan shrieked, but the first one to arrive was West, a medical kit in his hand. He threw it hotly onto the cot.

"What are you doing in my room? How *dare* you come into my room!"

Cain arrived and switched on the light; he was surprised to find Megan standing beside the refrigerator, trembling. He took a step into the room, West craning around him.

"Daniel, I *thought* I was renting a private room!"

"You are."

Cain faced Megan. He was by nature a diplomat, but this blatant invasion of sovereignty had placed matters well beyond arbitration.

"Meg, what the hell are you doing in here?"

West shouldered his way around him. "Never mind that. Would you please leave *now!*"

"Easy, Herbert, I'll take care of this. Meg? C'mon, hon, let's go."

"Dan-" She began to sob. "Dan, it's... it's Rufus!"

"Rufus? Where?"

Pointing, she replied, "In the fridge!"

Dubious until he noticed the sudden timidity in West's eyes, Cain strode over. There, stuffed flat between a jar of yellow liquid and something swaddled in paper toweling, was the cat. It was stiff and unmoving, its tail dangling from the shelf, its black coat uncharacteristically ragged.

"Daniel, I was going to show you-"

"Shut up!" Cain cut him off, bending and putting two fingers to the animal's neck. There wasn't a trace of life. Sniffing back tears, he rose and faced his boarder.

"What happened?"

"What do you think? It was dead when I found it."

"That's a lie," Meg charged through clenched teeth. "You killed him. He *hated* you."

"Don't be absurd! It suffocated. It knocked the garbage over, and it got its head stuck in a jar. You weren't home so I put it in the icebox. I certainly didn't think you'd want to find it just lying there. And frankly, did *not* want to stink the place up leaving it anywhere else."

"Then why didn't you call... or write a note?"

West grew agitated. "Forgive me, but I was busy pushing bodies around, as you well know. And what would a note have said? 'Cat dead, details later'?"

"West, *please*," Cain complained. His voice cracked with emotion, and his throat began to itch, reacting to something in the room, in the air.

"The point is, Daniel, I knew you were fond of it, and this seemed like the most sensible thing to do."

"You're lying." Megan's eyes blazed. "You killed him, I know you did."

"That's ridiculous, and also highly insulting,

Miss Halsey. As much as I don't care for people in my room, I care even less for unfounded accusations!"

"It *isn't* unfounded. Rufus was afraid of you."

"Was he? And when did he tell you this?"

"He didn't, not in words-"

"Telepathy, then?"

"All right," Cain interrupted, "that's enough. We're talking about my poor cat." Megan turned away from them both, and Cain glanced back at the refrigerator.

Seeing Rufus still and cold, he was still unable to accept his death. Cain was an infant when his parents were killed in a car accident, and no one else close to him had ever died. He felt as he had when they'd lost the young aerobics instructor. It wasn't like old age, where the biological machine wore down; the body had died, the system crashed, because one part had failed. It didn't seem right or fair. Bending to smooth down Rufus's fur, Cain noticed the yellow liquid. He'd never seen anything quite like it, neither medicine nor bodily fluid. His hand grew still, and West hastened forward. "Daniel, Miss Halsey - you're both upset, and I think it would be a good idea if you left... now."

Cain retrieved the vial. "What the hell's this?"

"*That* is none of your business."

West's indignation surprised him.

"If it's in my house, it's my business."

"I think not." He sneered at Megan. "Just as it's none of *my* business that you're sleeping with Dean Halsey's daughter."

"You bastard!" she snarled.

West ignored her. Grabbing the jar from Cain, he slipped it into his pocket and wagged a menacing finger. "You know, Daniel, I would not want to see a fellow student, especially one as promising as yourself, be thrown out of school, out of the profession, on moral grounds."

"Really? Well, for your information, I think Dr. Halsey just might understand."

West smiled mirthlessly. "You may be right. But the question is, are you sure you want to find out?"

Cain stiffened. "Are you *threatening* me?"

"A rather facetious charge, wouldn't you say, from someone who entered my room uninvited and went through my private belongings?"

Cain looked at Megan. West had him checkmated, and there was no point continuing the discussion. He took the young woman's hand.

"Touché," he muttered. "C'mon, Meg, let's take Rufus and get out of here."

West stepped in front of Cain. "Truce?" he pressed quietly. Cain nodded glumly. "Then I'll take care of the animal. It's the least I can do."

"I think *we* should do it," Megan countered.

"I believe Daniel has been through enough tonight. Why force him to endure this as well?"

Megan turned to her fiancé. "Dan?"

He sighed. "Herbert's right. I'd rather be alone with you right now than with poor Rufus."

Thanking him, Cain left, tugging Megan behind him. She lingered a moment, her eyes locking briefly with West's; she felt a chill, something that had nothing to do with Rufus but with West himself. Despite his neat appearance, he seemed dirty; *virulent* was the word that came to mind.

Slipping her arm around Cain's waist, she walked with him out into the cool October night. As they strolled beneath the old street-lamps and past even older buildings, Megan thought about what West had said - that Dan's career might be ruined if her father learned what they were doing. She wondered if marriage might be the answer to that, as well as to the problem of what to do with Herbert West. In the distance, a cat wailed; and though she knew it wasn't possible, Megan could have sworn it came from the house.

The cry ripped through Dan's sleep. He woke instantly and sat up, heart racing and eyes wide.

"Rufus?"

The shrill wail came again, and Cain swung from the bed. Pulling on trousers, he grabbed an old wooden Louisville Slugger and edged down the hall. There'd been bats when he first moved in, but they hadn't returned since he poisoned the few he'd found in the attic and nailed their carcasses to the outside wall. Bats might be blind, but they weren't stupid.

Still, that hadn't sounded like a bat. The cry was too loud, too deep, too ferocious. He checked the bathroom, poked the baseball bat against the metal grate of the ceiling ventilator. Nothing moved, and he continued edging down the hall.

"Herbert! Herbert, you hear that sound?"

When his roommate didn't answer, Cain rapped on the door.

"West? West!"

The shriek came again, this time from downstairs. It was followed by West's muted snarls.

"Vile... vile... thing!"

Cain put his cheek against the closed door. "West? What is that? What's going on?"

West screamed then, and Cain hurried down, stumbling in the darkness. Rising quickly, he bumped into the hooded light, which swung wildly.

In the bursts of light, he saw West squirming against a wall in the corner, something dark and ugly clinging to his back. Cain walked tentatively toward him, past a bridge table covered with chemicals and beakers. He saw West's eyes go wide.

"Cain, *get out of here!*"

"Herbert, what the hell is it?"

Just then a black object, vaguely round, rose behind West's neck; there was a flash of white, and West yelped. Whatever it was had bitten him - and also, apparently, punctured his pride.

"Cain - quick, get it off of me!"

Cain lunged forward, West turning and presenting his back. Cain still couldn't make out what the object was, but it squealed horribly when he clubbed it. The head craned back and bared its fangs. West seized the opportunity to fill his fists with the creature and tug it off. He hurled it, stiff-armed, across the room; the mass landed hard against an old highboy, behind which it quickly disappeared.

West scrambled to his feet and grabbed an old croquet mallet.

"Shit, Cain, *get* it!"

"West, what the hell is it?"

"Later! Later!"

West jabbed the mallet's rounded head behind the furniture, lunging with ever-longer thrusts.

"Cain, it's coming out the other side! Get it!"

"You want me to catch it?"

"I want you to break it's damn neck!"

The animal squealed when the mallet poked it; it fled out the other side, scampering behind a stack of cartons.

"Shit!"

"I'll get it," Cain said, tearing at the cardboard containers.

"No, there it goes - under the oil burner."

"Huh? It'll burn!"

West pursed his lips. "Not in this world."

Cain moved toward the old iron drum and was about to shove the bat beneath it when the animal leaped at him. The force of the blow surprised him, and he literally flew backward several feet, spilling into the cartons. The animal wrapped its arms and legs around his throat, the powerful claws digging into his flesh. West hurried over, and, pulling at the animal, they were able to rip it off. With a yell, Cain flung it hard to one side; the animal hit the concrete wall and stuck there for a moment, then slid slowly to the floor, leaving behind a dark smear of blood and entrails.

After feeling the puncture wounds at his throat and determining that they weren't severe, Cain hurried over to the carcass.

"Rufus! No..."

He turned on West, who backed slowly toward the cartons.

"What is this? What kind of *madness?*"

"Madness?" West laughed. "Are you *that* blind?" Suddenly, West's mouth fell open, and he pointed wildly. "Cain, behind you - look out!"

Cain spun, his bat at the ready. The cat's shadow moved in the swaying light, but the animal itself was still. When he turned back to West, the young man was leaning against the wall, giggling maniacally.

"Daniel, you're priceless! You jump for a dead cat and you call *me* mad."

Cain lowered the bat and stared in amazement, first at West and then at Rufus. Everything was dreamlike, surreal; he had to get upstairs, back to sanity.

Tugging a plastic sheet from the top of the highboy, Cain gently wrapped the cat within it and headed upstairs. He was determined to examine the animal and see exactly how it had died. After that, finding out just who was mad would be simple. If the cat hadn't suffocated and his roommate were playing some kind of game, then West was mad. He'd put him out the next morning, and that would be the end of it.

But if the cat *had* died in the trash, then Cain had problems.

Very *serious* problems.

Chapter 6

The two young men were bent over the table in West's room, the cat spread before them on the plastic sheet. Cain was still bare-chested, while West wore his tie and shirt, both garments blood-splattered. Cain was composed now and staring blankly at the cat, whereas West was agitated and in disarray, something wrong almost everywhere in his appearance: one brow was arched, the other straight; his mouth was twisted on one side, flat on the other; even his sleeves had been hastily rolled to uneven lengths.

Inwardly, however, the men were the opposite of what they appeared. Cain's brain was whirling with doubt and disbelief, while West's was a picture of reason itself.

"It's really quite simple," he explained patiently. "All life is a physical, magnetic and chemical process, correct? It stands to reason, that if one can find extremely fresh specimens and recharge that chemical process - bang, we have reanimation!"

"Your theory is not new, West."

He sat back on the stool. "But my reagent is. Even Gruber didn't have this mixture. He was a genius, but his feet were set on the wrong path, on recharging the brain through the circulatory system. He felt it was a more even means of distributing the compound, one which would provide less of a shock to the system. Unfortunately, that method also required a larger dose of the chemical, which was what killed him."

Cain faced him. "You mean he tried this on *himself?*"

West waved his hands from side to side. "That isn't important now. The point is, with the addition of certain buffers-phosphorus, mostly-"

"Which accounts for the yellow glow?"

"And also shepherds the reagent evenly to all corners of the brain. With my reformulation, I can reanimate the brain directly. Then *it* takes over, performing a system analysis and dispensing the remainder of the chemical exactly where it's needed for complete reactivation of the organism." He paused, his enthusiasm dampened. "But there's a problem." He pulled a notebook from a stack of papers on the floor and slid it before his companion. "Here... read!"

Cain opened the journal, forced his tired eyes to focus. "'With various animating solutions, I have killed and brought to animated life a number of rabbits, guinea pigs, cats, and dogs-'"

"I've broken the six-to-twelve-minute barrier," West interrupted excitedly. "I've conquered brain death."

Cain shook his head. "Herbert, what you've found is a way of making muscles expand and contract mechanically after death. We can do that now, with electricity."

"No!" West roared. "That is *not* what I have done!" He dragged his hands across his face, said tensely, "I expected more from you, Daniel. Please, just read on."

Cain resumed with a sigh. "'With the higher animals and the consequent increase in strength of the solution, the reaction has become more violent; unfortunately, even a fractional decrease in the size of the dosage fails to bring about any response. As Gruber had predicted it's all or nothing and, as a result, my research has become more difficult.'"

"You see, Daniel, what has happened is *not* rote restimulation. The brain and brain functions actually *do* return... but there's a *side effect*. Extreme trauma, and so far I haven't been able to find a way around it. Which is why I need you to help me."

"Help you? Are you mad?"

"Not at all. You are the *perfect* person to assist me. You're hard-working, bright, people respect you, and you have access to-certain authorities."

Cain looked up. "Dean Halsey?"

"He's a dull-witted man, but we can trust him, unlike that wretch Hill. Dean Halsey wants honor for his institution, and we can give it to him." He gripped Cain's forearm. "Daniel, do you realize what is at hand? We defeat death! We can achieve every doctor's dream! You'll be famous- and not just for one lifetime. If we succeed, you may very well live forever!"

Cain glanced at the book, flipping back through the pages. "You seem very confident, Herbert. I'm not. Not at all."

"I believe I mentioned when we first met that I'm always sure of what I say."

"The fact that you said it means diddly to me. And you didn't answer me before. You haven't done this... on people have you?"

West absently scratched the back of his neck and looked away, then around. "I've done all I can here. I'll need new lab space."

"Herbert, tell me the truth."

West looked back, his nostrils flaring. "I'll tell you what I *wish* to tell you until you agree to join me."

"In that case, you can keep your secrets."

West slapped the table so hard the cat bounced. "Dammit, Cain, you *will* help me!"

"No!"

"Why? Because it's - what was your trite expression? *Mad?*"

"No, Herbert, because frankly I don't believe you! I don't believe anything you've told me."

West's brow wrinkled, and he stretched both hands toward the cat. "How can you say that? You've seen the results!"

"I've also seen the hard-on you have for Dr. Hill, and you know what I think? I think you want to use me to get in good with Dean Halsey. That way you can embarrass Hill in some way, either screw around with his laser drill or-or I don't know what."

"You're tired, Daniel. You're not thinking clearly."

"I'm thinking *very* clearly, friend-at least, clear enough to know that Rufus wasn't dead to begin with. You drugged him and reduced his vital signs. You lowered his body temperature. He couldn't have been dead."

West studied his companion, then sat back. He nodded once, then slipped his hands beneath the cat. "Do you agree that he's dead now?" He let the animal thump on the table. "Answer me, Daniel. Do you agree that he's dead now?"

Reluctantly, Cain nodded.

"Fine."

West went to the refrigerator, withdrew the vial of formula, and fished the hypodermic from his medical bag.

Cain rose. "West, no. This is... *grotesque*."

"*Ignorance* is grotesque."

He filled the hypodermic halfway and

returned to the table. Cain pulled him back.

"West, stop!"

He squirmed away. "I'll show you, then you'll help me."

"No!"

"Yes you *will*, damn you. You're a man of science; it's time you started behaving like one."

West had a point, and, though he was loath to comply, Cain stood beside him as West bent over the bloody carcass. It couldn't work; he had examined the animal, which had not only suffocated but had lost most of its heart and all of one lung when it hit the wall.

"Science," West said solemnly. "A discipline designed to eliminate the unknown. The need to know, to explore; that is why I brought the infernal beast back to life in the first place."

Once again; Cain could not help but admire West's confidence, and he watched with unwilling fascination as his roommate placed the needle directly behind the cat's left ear.

"You really inject it directly into the brain?"

"Of course."

"But the needle - it would physically destroy the tissue."

"The formula compensates." West smiled. "Like a benevolent virus, it uses healthy cells to replicate itself; in this case, copying healthy cells to replace any which have been damaged." He emptied the syringe and stood. "Don't expect it to tango, Daniel. It *has* a broken back."

Numb, Cain stared over West's shoulder. Almost at once, the animal's eyes opened, and its paws began to twitch.

"Oh-my-God."

"Wonderful, isn't it?"

The small head craned around, trembling

85

violently; the mouth pulled open wide, and Rufus mewed horribly.

"Herbert... Why is it making that noise?"

West smiled. "Birth is always painful."

Cain shook his head. "But it was *dead*-"

"Twice," West noted smugly. "And Daniel... you wanted to know about people. I think this will interest you enormously." Like a kid on Christmas morning, the enthusiastic West ran to the refrigerator and recovered the mass of paper toweling. Cradling it in his hands, he approached warily. "Before I show you this, Daniel, I must know. Are you with me?"

Cain looked anxiously from West to the cat mewing pitifully, then back to West.

"I - I don't know... God, this is all so insane!"

West looked on disapprovingly. "Still thinking with your heart and not your brain, eh? Well, no matter. This will persuade you, I'm sure of it."

Shoving the squirming cat to one side, West pulled over an empty tray and lay the towels inside. Then he neatly uncovered the brain.

Cain gasped. "West, what-"

"Come now, Daniel. Surely you recognize the human brain."

"Yes, but where did it come from?"

"Dr. Hill. He neglected it," West replied, "when he left yesterday's class in a huff."

Cain felt weak. "Oh, Christ, West, it's her. The woman we lost the other morning... Wendy."

West looked up excitedly. "You know exactly when she died?"

He nodded.

"Tell me, man! It was early in the day, wasn't it?"

"A few minutes before noon," Cain answered numbly. "I can check Mace's log."

"As I thought," West repeated, tapping his chin. "Not as fresh a specimen as I'd have liked, but fresh enough to explain what happened."

"What... happened?"

"You'll see."

West went about his work gleefully, refilling the syringe and poking it into the gray mass. Almost at once, the brain began to wriggle from side to side like a Jell-O mold, Cain reflected.

"Herbert, this can't be! The brain can't be in pain like Rufus, it has no feeling!"

"Not for *physical!* pain," West pointed out. "Don't you realize what this is? The brain is emotionally alive; it wasn't *ready* to die. You've read about poltergeists, about the dead that refuse to accept their death. That is precisely what we're witnessing here! It's what Hill stole from Professor Gruber, the search for the soul, the seat of human life. It is here in the brain, Daniel. Do you understand? We have the power to rekindle life!"

Cain thought he was going to retch as he watched the woman's brain shake so hard it actually crept across the pan. So intently was he watching the brain that he'd forgotten about the cat and was utterly unaware of Megan as she entered the room. The first hint they had of her presence was when she howled a lung-ripping scream.

"*It's him!* Jesus, Dan, it's Rufus! *How-how?!*"

"Megan, what are you doing here?"

His own discomfort forgotten, Cain went to the young woman and escorted her from the room, leading her out into the fresh morning air. The shrieks quickly turned to moans and then to quiet sobbing. Inside, the cat had also quieted, the small dose of formula finally wearing off; glaring angrily out the door, West ignored the slippery agitation of the brain.

"Damn her!"

The last thing they needed was for Dean Halsey's daughter to tell her father what had transpired. Her frantic recital would quickly undo whatever credibility and reason Cain could bring to the case; he would have to leave then, and quickly, lest someone connect these experiments with what had happened to Professor Gruber back in Switzerland.

Because it was already two days dead, the brain would be nearly useless to him. West dumped the still-jiggling mass into the wastebasket, followed it with the cat. Pulling out the liner, he tied it shut and, laying it aside, flopped onto the cot.

It had been a long day, and he was exhausted.

Setting his wristwatch to wake him in two hours, West knew there was only one way to resolve the matter of the troublesome Megan Halsey. Either her father would cooperate willingly, or he'd cooperate unwillingly. But cooperate he would, providing West with the resources and autonomy he required.

West fell asleep just as the trash-bag, too, stopped shaking. Outside, the birds welcomed the morning, and traffic began to collect on Hazard Weeden Boulevard; it was the start of another ordinary weekday in sleepy Arkham, Massachusetts.

Chapter 7

"Sir, Herbert West has effected re-animation in dead animal tissue."

Seated in a plush armchair beside Dean Halsey's desk, Cain did not quite believe the words as they passed from his own lips. Halsey's expression showed that he didn't believe them either, his mouth drooping at the edges, brow furrowing painfully beneath the neatly brushed white hair. But there was something else in his expression, in his reserve - something dark and unpleasant.

"Mr. Cain, I'm surprised. In the three years I've known you, I thought you were above juvenile pranks."

"Dean Halsey, this isn't a prank. I've *seen* it! He brought back a dead animal, a cat - brought it back to life!"

Halsey continued signing correspondence as if he hadn't heard Cain speak. "No, I hadn't expected such nonsense from you, Mr. Cain, but I should have guessed it when you took up with Mr. West."

Cain leaned across the desk. "Look, I know he's unstable, but I've seen the results! For that matter, so has your daughter."

Damn! He'd said it without thinking and

braced himself for the inevitable. The Dean tossed his glasses aside.

"Did she? Which brings up an interesting question, young man. Just what have you been doing with my daughter?"

"Studying, sir."

"Is that all? You haven't involved Megan in your insanity?"

"No, sir. Well, not exactly involved. She forgot her book and came by this morning... She walked in on an experiment. I never *intended* to involve her."

Halsey folded his hands and stared at them, his fingers white around the knuckles. "Tell me, then. In what way *are* you involved with her?"

Cain swallowed hard. "As you know, sir, we... study together."

"Medicine or each other?"

The young man ached to answer truthfully, to say that his daughter was a woman of twenty, that they were in love and intended to marry, that what they did in private was their business and not his. But he also wanted to retain his membership in the student body, and, remembering Megan's words, "the last of the Puritans," he said nothing.

"As I thought," the older man snorted.

"Pardon?"

Halsey retrieved his bifocals and rested them on his nose.

"Your silence is answer enough."

In his most official tones, he said, "Tomorrow morning you will submit to me a written apology for this entire affair. These *experiments*" - *he* spat out the word - "were clearly beyond the scope of your legitimate studies, and, judging from your presence here instead of in Dr. Hill's class, they've obviously interfered with your ability to do your classwork. If any equipment from the hospital or from the laboratories of Miskatonic University were involved in any of this unauthorized activity, criminal charges may be pressed. You will in any case have your student loan rescinded."

The young man stared in shock. "My loan? But sir, I won't be able to continue school."

"As for Mr. West," Halsey went on, "he need submit no apology. Last night at dinner, Dr. Hill told me what transpired in class. You may tell your brash roommate that he may continue his research without the impediment of an education. As of now, he is no longer a student at this university."

"But that's ridiculous - he's worked a scientific miracle!" Halsey's face grew ruddy, but Cain didn't care; whatever the outcome, he had to see this through. "Please, can we just discuss this? I think you're being blinded by your emotions."

"And *you're* being impertinent!"

Cain stared past Halsey and tried to compose himself. He regarded all the framed degrees, the honors, the parchments; they were meaningless. Halsey was revealing himself to be as narrow and vindictive a man as ever lived.

"Sir-"

"That will be all, Mr. Cain."

"All? All for what, this auto-da-fe? Megan tried to warn me, but I didn't believe you'd really come down on me just because I was seeing her!"

"Mr. Cain!"

"I'm sorry, but you're making a terrible mistake-"

"I think not!" Halsey rose, his barrel chest inflat-ing beneath his three-piece suit. "The only mistakes I seem to have made of late were admitting Mr. West to our school... and allowing you to see my daughter." He sat heavily, resumed his writing. "Good morning, young man."

Cain stood slowly and looked down at the desk, at the brass scales of justice; they were filled with paper clips and the odd rubber band. "Don't take this out on Meg," he said quietly. "She tried to stop me."

Halsey yanked off his glasses and flagged them at Cain. "I *said* that will be all - unless you care to join Mr. West looking for a new place to further your studies."

"No, sir."

His eyes on the centuries-old Persian rug, Cain left the Dean's office, ignoring the covert stare of the secretary as he passed. He didn't know which troubled him more, losing his tuition or having to face West with the bad news. Over breakfast, West had been buoyed by his progress and didn't see how Halsey could fail to give them financing and laboratory space. For that matter, neither did Cain.

"Being angry about someone dating his baby," Cain reflected. "That's how."

West was still at the house, having skipped Hill's class; he took all the news without comment, though his jaw tensed noticeably when he learned of his expulsion. For Cain's part, he was disappointed by the morning's events, though not as much as he thought he'd be. On entering the house, he'd seen a huge spider he could have sworn he'd sprayed the day before. West's work, compounded by his queer manner, were making him paranoid.

West shut himself in his room while Cain had some coffee, changed the bandages on his clawed upper back, reviewed his finances - he had two weeks to come up with a battle plan before his tuition was due - and made ready to go on his rounds with Dr. Harrod. Bundled in an old leather jacket, his battered medical kit under his arm, he was about to leave when West came up to him.

"Daniel," he said, "do you intend to take this lying down?"

Cain jammed his hands into his pockets. "No. But first I want to talk to Megan about it, see what she thinks."

West's smile was pinched. "Of course. Tell me, when are you through with your rounds?"

"Around half past eleven. Why?"

"Fine. Can you meet me" - West touched his nose thoughtfully - "at the service elevator, in the basement?"

"I guess so." Cain shrugged once. "But why?"

West laid a hand on his shoulder. "Because, Daniel, unlike you, I fully intend to take *my* next step lying down. See you at eleven-thirty."

His step unusually buoyant, West returned to his room. Walking out into the brisk October breeze, Cain had a feeling he wouldn't be taking Professor Streaman's exam that afternoon, which was just as well. He never *had* finished reading about spirochetal jaundice...

The creak of the wheels was unusually loud - or was it just his imagination? - as Cain pushed the table down the corridor. Was it also his imagination that the table seemed heavier, that the orderlies he passed were eyeing it - and him - with suspicion? Was Dr. Hill just tired when they passed him, or had there been something else in his gaze, something ominous?

He cursed West for ever having entered his life.

Genius or not, this was no longer the era of Jennings and Curie. Researchers had to play the game, had to be politicians and diplomats as well as geniuses. At worst, they had to obey public laws, which meant that they didn't go skulking down university corridors disguised as corpses.

He glared at the bare feet of the corpse, at the toe tag which read "L. A. Zarus." The name had been West's touch, a bit of defiance. It was insane, he knew, just as the entire undertaking was mad; but West was right. Seeing is believing, and right now their options were few.

Cain wondered if Mace would notice the sweat collecting on his upper lip.

The guard waved once and stood. "They keep on coming, don't they?" he said around his fat cigar.

"Oh yeah. They're just dyin' to get in."

Dan wiped his palms on his hospital greens and waited while the big man unlocked the door. Pocketing the key ring, he came over and lifted the top of the sheet.

"Say, Cain; you ain't got my dinner under there, have ya?"

Dan hastily pushed the sheet back down. "Yeah, Mace. One meatball run over by a semi."

Mace's brow knit tightly above his nose. "Oooooh... I think I lost my appetite."

"You, Mace?"

As much as he wanted to get in and out of the morgue, Cain also wanted to keep up the conversation, create an air of normalcy. He rolled the cart in slowly; he was about to tap "L. A. Zarus" on the shoulder when Mace swung in.

"Say, you gonna be around for a while?"

"Yeah, sure." He choked, but Mace didn't seem to notice.

"Mind keepin' an eye on the store while I get some coffee?"

"Not at all. Take your time."

Mace thanked him and ambled down the

corridor. When he was gone, Cain locked the double doors; hearing the telltale click, the body on the table rose and threw off the sheet.

"Meatball?"

"Just put your shoes on, Herbert, it was nothing personal."

While West tugged on his socks, Cain reached under his smock and pulled a flashlight from his hip pocket. Turning on the lights, he headed for the metal door to the morgue. Hearing footfalls in the hallway, Cain froze, motioning West to do likewise; when the footsteps passed, Cain let out a tremulous breath.

"Damn! We can *still* get caught!"

West was tying his shoes. "And what will they do? Embalm us?"

Cain stretched to relieve the tacky discomfort under his arms. "Only if they're feeling merciful. Herbert, will you come *on.*"

West rolled down the sleeves of his blue shirt and hopped from the table. He followed Cain into the morgue, then pulled out his own penlight and darted to the nearest body. It was Christmastime again, Cain reflected, and he tried hard to remain aloof.

West read from the toe tag. "Burn victim. She may fall apart on us."

"Spare me the critiques."

West snorted. "Some doctor you'll make."

"I'll be a fine doctor," Cain rejoined. "I just wasn't cut out to be a graverobber."

West was already bending over the next body in line, the toes of which were charred stubs. "Here's your meatball," he snickered, then scuttled over to the third. "Shotgun wound to the head. Even a bath of formula wouldn't work on this one."

Shivering from the cold of the dark, refrigerated room, Cain had slipped around to the fourth. "Oh, God-rotten!"

"Must be the old lady they found in the marsh. I read about it in the obituaries." West examined another. "Malpractice. Let's leave this one, in case it's Hill."

Cain glanced toward the outer doors. "C'mon, Herbert, the clock's running!"

West stood, tapping his toe impatiently, casting his light anxiously about. "Wait!" He dashed toward the back of the room, Cain in tow. West studied the tag. "Yes, I think you read about him as well. He arrived early this morning. John Doe. Apparently just dropped dead." West plucked off the sheet and dropped it to the floor. He quickly examined the scalp and then the chest. "No record of any damage. Almost perfect!"

Cain looked on. "Why 'almost'?"

"He's got a cracked rib, probably broken when he fell. There could be heart damage."

"Then let's find another one. We can't afford to blow this."

"No! We do not have time, you said so yourself!" He fished the vial from one pocket, the hypodermic from another. "Besides, *almost* perfect is good enough. All we need tonight is a specific, conscious reaction. He's been dead for hours. *Any* evidence of reanimated consciousness will justify proceeding." He began filling the instrument barrel. "Start the recorder."

Cain's pulse was throbbing under his chin. "Start the damn recorder! Make the entry."

The young man snapped out of his stupor. They wouldn't get caught, and even if they did, what was the worst that could happen? If the body remained dead, no one could prove a thing. If it moved, there was no way Dean Halsey would carry out his threats. He gulped down his anxiety and wet his lips.

"October-"

"Tenth!" West snapped. "October tenth. Subject: male."

"Age?"

"Age-uh, early twenties."

"Physical condition?" West prompted impatiently.

Cain dragged his flashlight across the body. "Sub-ject appears to have been in excellent physical condition. Apparent cause of death-"

His teeth began to chatter, not entirely from the cold. "Uh, what was it?"

"Heart failure!"

"Right. Heart failure."

"Time," West glanced at his watch, "ten thirty three P.M."

Cain swallowed hard again, repeated the time into the micro-recorder.

"Dosage," said West, as he lifted the head and jabbed the needle into the base of the skull, "15 cc's."

Curiosity was again taking over, and Cain felt his queasiness subsiding. "Fifteen cc's of reagent being administered."

There were footsteps along the corridor, only this time they seemed far away. All that mattered was what was happening on the table before them.

"Time elapsed?"

Cain checked his watch. "Fifteen seconds."

"Something should have happened by now."

The footsteps faded.

"It's not working! Let's get out of here!"

West sucked on his upper lip. "Obviously, the human dosage factor is unknown. It worked on Gruber only because he had just died."

"It *what?!* West, you-murdered him?"

"Don't be naive, Daniel. Gruber took his life for the express purpose of testing the formula, just as I would have done for him. Unlike the people at this institution, he was a true scientist!" He snatched up the vial. "Obviously there is a geometric correlation between the dosage and the length of time the subject has been dead. This will help us to find that ratio." He poked the needle into the stopper. "Increasing the dosage... 20 cc's of reagent."

"Herbert, you're scatter-shooting. Let's go!"

"No! We need the data!"

Cain shook his head and reluctantly kept his light on the body while West administered the serum. Both men looked anxiously for a sign of life, shining their beams on the subject's lips, eyes, fingers.

After nearly a full minute, West greeted the continued stillness with a heartfelt oath.

Dean Halsey guided the Lincoln Continental down Kadath. Traffic was heavy because of the changing shifts at the Ogan plant. He punched the wheel when he got stuck behind a Rambler, then again when he was caught at a four-way light.

"I knew we should have sent for an ambulance. Remember how you loved to drive in them when we first came here?"

Beside him, Megan said nothing. She wiped away the mascara running down her tear-streaked cheeks and continued staring into her lap. Ordinarily, Halsey would have been unable to resist Megan's tears. But this was different. He had given Hill his assurance that the "matter" of Cain and West had been taken care of, and he'd been compromised. He hated to look like a fool, but he hated even more to have his grant magnet disturbed.

He squeezed the wheel. Why did she have to fall in love with a student instead of one of the young professors? He always invited them over for dinner with Hill, to make it look like business - and she resisted every one of them. Cain was a well-intentioned young man but naive; he would never make money, he'd end up in research, or in some Third World sewer like Megan's mother.

He didn't blame himself for Diana's leaving. A fellow professor, she'd walked out at the height of the campus protests in the sixties, offended by her husband's conservatism and feeling that needy Vietnamese children were more important than her own daughter. The last he'd heard, Diana had founded her own version of the Peace Corps in Afghanistan, helping the beleaguered rebels.

He didn't blame himself, but he knew what hardship the situation had caused for Megan. She'd lost her mother to activism, her friends in a succession of moves and her childhood because she'd willingly shouldered the role of housekeeper and hostess.

The intersection was blocked by an Ogan truck, so they sat out the green light where they were.

Halsey refused to look at Megan. She hadn't cried like this for so long, and her tears brought back memories. In his mind's eye she was seven again, and he was still teaching medicine at Connecticut University in Denver. She'd wanted a pony, and because he couldn't afford one he'd sold his coin collection in order to buy it. She'd been so excited that she named the animal Al in his honor. He could also see her clearly when she was nine and the delivery crew had wheeled the piano in. At the teacher's conference, Miss Ackerman had said that Megan showed musical aptitude, so he freelanced at night proofreading medical textbooks in order to purchase a piano. It had been his own mother's favorite instrument, and, though he could only afford a used upright, Megan made it sound like a Steinway. She titled her first composition "Al's Song."

Today, very little gave Halsey more pleasure than to watch Megan ride or listen to her play. Making these things possible were the right sacrifices to have made.

Their lives together had been give and take, but this time Megan would have to give. It hurt to deny her anything, but he couldn't let her make a mistake of this magnitude. Cain was merely adequate for her before; he was dead wrong for her now. His medical career was finished, and Halsey would not have his daughter marry a nobody.

The traffic began to move, and Halsey cut out around the Rambler.

"Daddy, why can't you understand that he loves me?"

"I do understand," he said calmly, "but you have to understand that Daniel Cain is wrong for you."

"Why? Because he isn't one of those asshole snob professors you keep trying to push on me?"

"Megan—"

"Don't baby me, Daddy! Even if you throw him out, I'll go with him. We're going to get married!"

Halsey felt his neck muscles tense, but he refused to yell. Megan was distraught, and, besides, he had the upper hand. He had to show magnanimity in victory.

"You're doing no such thing. These other suitors may be... snobs, some of them, but they're all stable, intelligent men."

"They're all little Dean Halseys, which may be what *you* want for me, but it isn't what *I* want for me!"

"Stop it, Megan! We're not talking about a pony now, we're talking about a lifetime commitment."

"Exactly! And I want Dan. Whatever his

100

faults, he'll grow up. We'll grow *together*."

Halsey shook his head. "I'm afraid you won't have the chance. Mr. Cain is facing more than expulsion. He may be facing criminal charges as well. Carl says he heard Cain and Mr. West in the morgue."

"That's because they're scientists, Daddy. You should sympathize with that! Whatever Dan is doing, I'm sure he has a good reason-"

"The reason, honey, is that Daniel Cain is mad. I've seen this happen to medical students before - good ones! Too much pressure and they crack!"

Megan pounded the dashboard. "Don't you see, Daddy, it's West! He's the one who's mad."

"Then it's contagious, because after what I heard this afternoon-"

"You mean Rufus?" she demanded.

"I mean that rubbish about the cat. Not only has Cain seen dead cats come back to life, he's convinced you that you saw them too."

"But I *did!* Rufus was dead, and then he was alive!"

Halsey swung the car into the employees' parking lot and pulled into his spot. He punched a button, unlocking the doors, then regarded his daughter.

"You only *thought* the cat was alive. West tricked you, just as he tricked Daniel. Carl's right. He did it so the college would give him money and resources. But he's not getting them, and Daniel Cain is not getting them either. What's more, Daniel Cain also is not getting you."

"He's already had me," she pouted.

Halsey froze. Megan had wanted to hurt him, but she was unprepared for the utter desolation that filled his eyes. Numbly, he opened the door and stepped out, padding slowly toward the entrance, oblivious to the greeting of the guard and the orderlies he passed.

Megan snatched the keys from the ignition and hurried after him. "Daddy, wait! You don't understand!"

Halsey paid her no attention. His step quickening, face becoming redder, gait becoming angrier as he walked, he made for the head nurse's station. Dr. Harrod was seated there, having a snack, and he closed on her like a shark.

"Grace, what the hell are you doing here?"

She looked at him indignantly and answered through a mouthful of donut. "I'm filling in while Jan's in the lavatory."

"Not very well, I hear."

"I beg your pardon?"

"I just got a call from Carl Hill. Would you happen to know if Mr. Cain is on the loose in this hospital?"

"He's in the morgue, I think."

"You *think*? Isn't the person at this desk supposed to *know* where hospital personnel are?"

"Allan, I'm a doctor, not a receptionist! All I know is what Mace told me when I bumped into him in the cafeteria."

"Mace? And what was *he* doing away from his post?"

"He said something about Cain having relieved him."

Halsey pounded the desk just as Megan ran up. Dr. Harrod noticed her bloodshot eyes, understood at once what had caused her father's mood. Although Harrod was glad she hadn't accepted Halsey's marriage proposal years before, she felt badly for Megan. Her father was ill equipped to raise anything but funds.

"I'll have that bastard's job!" Halsey vowed,

turning his back on his daughter as she ran up. "I specifically told Dr. Riley to suspend Cain and have Mace take him off the floor if he reported for work."

"Allan, Dr. Riley has been in emergency surgery for four hours. I haven't seen him, and I'm sure Jan hasn't either."

"Then he should have left word!"

"Why - is there a problem?"

"Problem?" Halsey snickered. "There's no problem, as long as the deceased of Arkham have some *very* understanding next-of-kin." Halsey looked down the hall. "Hold that elevator!" He turned to Dr. Harrod. "Grace, would you please page Mr. Cain and have him report to the level L security desk. And whatever you do" - he regarded his daughter - "make sure that *she* stays right here."

"You can't stop me," Megan sobbed. "I followed you here, and I'm going to follow you until you listen to me."

He turned on her, the hurt that had been in his eyes replaced with fury. "You're going to stay *right here*, young lady. You won't see him *or* sleep with him again!"

Several people in the waiting room turned to stare. Dr. Harrod looked down at her coffee.

"You can't do this, Daddy. I love him!"

Noticing the many eyes upon them, Dean Halsey recomposed himself and bent closer to Megan. Under cover of Dr. Harrod's announcement, he said in a rough whisper, "I don't care! You're my daughter, and you'll do as you're told - if not for your own sake, then for that of Mr. Cain."

"What do you mean?"

"If you do what I tell you, things will go much easier for Mr. Cain. If not-"

He didn't have to finish. Megan's shoulders

slumped, and Dr. Harrod came from behind the desk. She took Megan lightly by the arm.

"Sit down, Miss Halsey."

Megan sat in a swivel chair and watched as her father hurried down the hall. Her lower lip quivered. "It's blackmail," she whimpered. "My own father blackmailing me."

"University Deans and professors are very good at that," Harrod said, offering Megan her coffee. The young woman shook her head, and Harrod took a sip. "I know what you're going through, but Mr. Cain will be up soon, and we can discuss it then."

"Why bother? Daddy doesn't understand. He just won't let go!"

"Daddies are very good at that," Harrod said sagely.

Megan stared helplessly as her father scuttled down the corridor toward the elevator. Half rising, she yelled suddenly, "Don't blame him, Daddy! It's West! It's all West!"

Chapter 8

The two men stood in the dark of the room, staring down at the spotlighted corpse. The big John Doe lay still, his lantern jaw and powerful hands unmoving. The dragon tattoo on his right arm seemed more alive than his own stiff limbs.

"We've failed!" Cain sighed.

West slapped the corpse roughly. "He failed, not I"

"That doesn't matter right now. Come on, let's go. Someone will be coming any minute!"

Even before he'd finished uttering the warning, Cain heard the announcement over the loudspeaker. *"Mr. Daniel Cain, please report to the security desk, level L. "*

"Oh, God."

Cain looked at the inanimate body. He deserved what he got. Any number of things could have explained the cat, the brain. How could he have been so stupid? In his eagerness to want to believe, he had blundered into disaster.

"Cover him up," Cain said with disgust. "Let's go."

West stood staring at the corpse, studying it. A thousand thoughts raced through his mind. John Doe looked like a biker. Was there too much dust in his lungs? Drugs in his veins? Gas fumes - had they done him in?

"I said let's go!"

"All right!" West snapped, grabbing the sheet and tossing it over the body. "I just don't understand. It should have worked"

Cain helped him straighten the sheet, neither man noticing the fingers of the corpse's right hand flick once, then again.

"The girl's brain had been dead longer, and that came back."

The entire arm twitched.

Cain had no desire to discuss the matter. All he wanted was to get home and get stoned. And call Megan, if he could find the courage. He hadn't seen her all day and wasn't sure he wanted to hear how she couldn't marry him now that he was on the verge of being kicked out of school.

Cain heard the popping and felt the spray of blood on his neck at the same time.

"What the hell?"

Turning, he saw the corpse sitting up on the table, its joints snapping as they defied rigor mortis. Its arms were stretched rigidly before it, speckled with blood which was gushing in violent spurts from its mouth; the eyes, open wide, were glazed and dry.

West's eyes ignited with delight. "Do you see, Daniel? Do you *see*?"

"I see-"

West slapped Cain hard on the back. "Didn't I tell you it would work? Quick, the recorder!"

Cain pulled it from his pocket, fumbled to turn the device on. "Time?"

"Ten thirty-four forty-eight."

Cain murmured the time, then described what

was happening as, groaning, the corpse slid from the table and staggered several stiff-legged steps. It bent slightly, momentarily to its right.

"Astonishing!" West blurted. "It's aware of the broken rib!"

"Does it feel pain?" Cain asked.

"Impossible to tell. We'll have to do specific tests. Come on."

With Cain at his heels, West slowly approached the naked zombie. He was crouching slightly, his hands open in a calming gesture. The corpse regarded him for a moment, then snarled. Blood spattered over West's glasses.

"Easy... " West said. "We want to help you." Turning slowly toward the table, the zombie sud-denly grabbed it and, with superhuman strength, threw it across the room. Then it grabbed the nearest body and did likewise, the corpse bouncing off the wall like a rag doll. Another table followed, sending the young medics to the floor.

"Shit!" Cain swore. "What's wrong?"

"Shock, confusion - I'm not sure! Just *grab* it." Rising, the young men charged the zombie as it turned to grab another table; they both yelped as, with ease, the corpse grabbed their upper arms and twisted hard. It released Cain but not West; taking the young man by the shoulders, it heaved him backward across a row of tables and into the wall.

Scrambling over a pair of up-ended carts, Cain helped West to his feet.

"What now?"

West stood and adjusted his glasses. He regarded the corpse, which had just climbed atop a female cadaver.

"Stop!" he yelled. "Just... *stop!*"

The corpse froze, then climbed down slowly.

"There," West said giddily. "It listened to me! We must have startled it before, that's all."

With a startling roar, the zombie ran at them, batting Cain aside with its shoulder and squeezing West around the waist. The bear hug brought a quick crimson flush to the young man's face, and he slammed futilely on his captor's head and neck.

"Dan!" he wailed. "Daaaaaan!"

The young man rose and picked up a pair of wheels which had snapped off one of the tables. Bracing himself against the door, he threw them at the brute's back; the zombie turned and, with a roar, barreled toward Cain, who jumped out of its way.

Out in the corridor, Halsey heard the commotion and ran forward. Swearing at Mace's empty desk, he rushed in and tried the door to the morgue. It was locked, and he pounded heavily with the side of his fist.

"Cain, what's going on? What's all that ruckus?"

There was a clanging of metal, the moaning of one man, and the curses of another.

"Cain? Cain! Open the door!" Halsey put his ear to the metal. He heard low, feral snarling. "Is West in there with you? You're in a lot of trouble, both of you!"

The door came down with a crash. Halsey shrieked as he fell beneath it. The zombie crawled across it and leaped up and down across the top. There was an audible cracking of bones in Dean Halsey's chest.

Hearing snapping and Halsey's pitiful cries, the zombie scurried to one side. It flung the door from its victim and scooped the stunned Halsey up under its arms. Holding him high, it smashed the Dean repeatedly against a chalkboard. When the dazed man tried to push the zombie away, the creature simply took his pinkie and ring finger between its teeth and snapped them off. Halsey wailed as his spurting blood mingled with the red on the corpse's chin, though his cries were higher and more agonized than those of the zombie.

Spitting the fingers out, the corpse heaved Dean Halsey across the room. The man tumbled from the wall to a countertop to the floor. He made a weak effort to crawl toward the door before the monster was once more upon him. The zombie picked him up again just as Cain and West came running from the morgue.

"Oh, God," Cain muttered. "It's Dean Halsey!"

Racing over, he locked his fists and began striking the monster on the back and head.

"Stop! For God's sake, *stop!*"

"That's it, Daniel, keep it busy!" West advised as he grabbed a table leg and hurried over to a medicine chest. Smashing the glass, he returned with a bone saw.

"Okay, Dan," he said, starting the instrument up. "Look out."

Cain backed away while West, a grim expression on his bruised face, stepped behind the zombie. Locking one arm around its neck, he pressed the spinning blade to its back. The zombie shot erect as the saw cut through its spine, but West held on. Like a rodeo bronco the zombie stomped, snarling, around the room, West's feet rarely touching the floor. When the blade finally emerged from its chest, it stared down with a puzzled expression at the metal which was spinning blood and chunks of its heart around the room. Then it dropped, without a sound, and West slowly withdrew his forearm from the zombie's chest cavity.

"No," he said dryly to Cain, "they feel no

pain." The thing was too surreal to be sickening; Cain just stared in amazement as, tossing the bone saw aside, West threw clinging viscera from his hand and hurried over to where Halsey lay crumpled in a corner.

"He's dead."

Cain turned away; all he could think about was Megan and what this would do to her. He sank slowly to the floor beside a stool, trying to imagine what he would tell her.

West began dragging Halsey from the corner by his feet. "Come on, Daniel, find the recorder!"

Cain looked up. He realized, in an instant, what West intended to do. Now he felt his stomach churning.

"Herbert... no!"

West gestured wildly at the John Doe. "Did you see him, Daniel? He listened to me! He made a conscious act!"

"You're wrong! He heard you as an animal would. He'd have murdered his own mother."

West used his tie to wipe smears of blood from his glasses. "Well... you may be right. It had probably been dead too long, it wasn't fresh enough. We probably only revived the senses and the instincts. Come on..." - he pointed toward Halsey's head - "help me get him up."

Cain laughed miserably. "You can't be serious."

"I am, Daniel. Will you give me a hand here?"

"No! I'm not going to let you experiment on him. Christ, this man was almost my father-in-law."

"He still can be! Look, this man was a short-sighted son of a bitch, one who interrupted an important experiment in progress! Granted, it was an accident, but he *owes* us. Besides" - West picked up Halsey's wrist and rubbed the flesh between his fingers

- "this is the freshest body we could come across short of killing one ourselves. Please, Daniel, every moment we spend talking about it costs us results! Will you give me a hand?"

Cain lay his head against the stool, made no move toward the body. West tried and failed to lift Halsey himself. He came over again, on his knees.

"Don't you understand what I'm saying? *We can bring him back to life!*"

Cain regarded West coldly. "Like Gruber?"

"No, not like Gruber! Like Dean Allan Halsey, God help him! All right, Daniel - never mind me, never mind him. You're an idealist, what about patients?"

"Patients?"

"Yes, the ones enduring twelve hundred heart transplants each year, eight thousand kidney transplants! We can stop that suffering, and also the pirates who are getting two hundred thousand dollars for complete cadavers for these operations. And what about you and Miss Halsey? Are you prepared to tell her that we were indirectly responsible for her father's death?"

Cain considered these points. He didn't think for a moment that West cared about patients or about Megan - but *he* certainly did. And, he wondered, how much worse could they possibly make things by trying?

He climbed to his feet. "All right, damn you. Let's do it."

With a mad smile, West scooped up Halsey's feet while Cain took his shoulders. Together they hoisted him onto the table.

"Get the recorder and find my serum," West ordered as he used the straps to lash Halsey to the tabletop.

Cain headed for the morgue and returned with the recorder and the vial. He handed the latter to

111

West. West fondled it with relief. "Ah… good. Thank God for unbreakable plastic, one of man's few durable inventions!" He sneered at Halsey's corpse as he readied the injection. "It's certainly more durable than *this*. But we'll soon take care of that, won't we, Daniel?" He bent over the prone subject and lifted his head. "Won't we, Dean Halsey?" He motioned for Cain to bring the recorder over. "Twelve cc's being administered, the dosage lessened in accordance with the freshness of the sub-ject."

Cain stood numbly across the table, gazing down at Halsey's blood-streaked face, the clotted tangle of white hair, the ripped vest and rumpled jacket. The indignity of death once again angered and sickened him. Narrow-minded as Dean Halsey was, he'd been a poised, distinguished man; he deserved better than to end up a gored mass on a stainless-steel table.

As though reading Cain's mind, West observed, "Amazing, isn't it, that such a fastidious man should make his greatest contribution to science in a state of utter disarray?" He cackled. "Can't you just *see* the photos in the *New England Journal of Medicine?*"

"Herbert, please…"

Cain didn't care whether it was nerves or vindictiveness that was causing West to gloat. For all his flaws, the Dean deserved a modicum of respect, of dignity.

Laying the empty hypodermic aside, West crouched so that he and Halsey were eye to eye. The levity was gone from his eyes and from his manner. His chin was outthrust, his brow brooding, his taut lips inches from Halsey's ear.

"Five seconds. Come on, you old bastard."

Cain knew, of course, that Halsey *would* be coming back. It might take another shot-in-the-dark overdose, but West would bring him around. For the

Dean's sake - for Megan's sake -he quietly prayed that Halsey would be more cooperative than their last subject.

"Ten seconds."

Cain heard himself being paged again. The commander was dead, but the army fought on.

"Fifteen seconds. Come on, I'll show *you!*"

West's voice was sharp, impatient. Curious as he was, Cain laid the cassette recorder on the table, then swung away and sank to the floor. If Dean Halsey came back like John Doe, he didn't want to see it. He didn't want that image of horror seared into his brain.

"Sixteen... seventeen. Come *on!*"

West slammed his fist on the table, and Halsey's eyes popped open. There were two loud intakes of air - that of Halsey and that of West - after which the young scientist began talking excitedly.

"Seventeen seconds - reanimation at seventeen seconds! The eyes opened - breathing regular. Pulse" - he seized the man's wrist, counting to himself - "pulse forty but strong. Slight expectoration of blood, possibly from a laceration of the tongue."

Cain hesitated. He was listening carefully to Halsey's breathing, which was hollow, watery. There was blood in his mouth. Was there blood in the windpipe as well? In the lungs? His eyes sought out the bone saw as he waited.

If West were aware of the Dean's strained breath, he made no mention of it.

"Subject apparently confused and tugging at restraining straps-but not as violent as last subject. God, Daniel, I've done it! He's alive! He's *alive!* Dean... Dean Halsey!" West put his lips to the man's ear. "I want you to hear this, Dean. You once did me a favor by admitting me into your medical school. Well, sir," he clucked triumphantly, "consider the debt paid - with interest. Welcome back to life!"

Megan had moved to a waiting-room bench situated halfway between the nurse's station and the elevators. Though she was flipping through the *Ladies' Home Journal*, her eyes kept shifting between Dr. Harrod and the clock. It had been nearly a half-hour since her father had left, yet they were still paging Cain. She hoped her lover hadn't done something rash.

The minutes dragged as Megan waited for her caretaker to become involved with someone or to leave the desk; for nearly a half-hour now she'd simply signed forms, talked on the phone - and looked frequently at Megan.

Suddenly, a nurse came jogging up to the desk.

"Dr. Harrod, we need you in the crash room."

The doctor looked from the nurse to Megan. "Coming," she said after a moment's hesitation, then disappeared down the hall.

Sighing, Megan flipped the magazine aside and scooted toward the bank of elevators. She took the first one going anywhere, just to get off the main floor; as it happened, the carriage was headed for the basement.

Her companion, old Dick Ankles, the janitor, tipped his hat and headed to the left, toward the boiler room. The corridor before her was deserted, and Megan proceeded cautiously.

West was shining his penlight in Dean Halsey's eyes when he heard the elevator door slide open.

Megan called out. "Dan? Are you down here?"

West swore. "Damn that bitch!"

Cain became alert. "Meg?"

Dean Halsey groaned. His voice was not

articulate, but there was enough control and variation in the tones to bring a broad smile to West's lips.

"Daniel, do you hear that? He's actually trying to speak to his daughter!"

"Dan? Daddy?"

Cain filled with dread. "Herbert, what if he thinks we're going to hurt her?"

"Pardon?"

While West looked on, puzzled, Halsey's eyes rolled back into his head, and, with a roar, he popped his straps. West fell back from the table, but Cain was not so lucky. The reanimated corpse locked its powerful fingers around his throat and began lifting him from the floor. Cain gurgled helplessly as the man's manicured nails dug into his flesh. "Don't worry," West shouted hopefully. "He only has three fingers on that one!"

"Herbert!" Megan yelled. "Is that you? Is Dan all right?"

West's face screwed unpleasantly as he finally grasped Cain's warning. "Miss Halsey, just shut up and stay away!" he shouted as he jumped to his feet. Running to help his colleague, West was snared by Halsey's free hand; the corpse literally dragged him across the table by his neck, bringing both men to their knees on either side of him. He sat up, oblivious to West flailing at his arm and Cain trying desperately to pry his remaining fingers loose.

"I've had enough orders for one day!" Megan protested as she stepped into the doorway. The young woman's expression shaded from defiance to rage, and she ran in. "No, Daddy! What are you doing!?"

Dean Halsey looked over, his mouth falling open dumbly. Hastily releasing the students, he rolled from the table and loped awkwardly to a corner of the room, where he crawled beneath a large sink and crouched, trembling, his back to the room.

Megan walked slowly toward him while Cain, rubbing his throat, ran to intercept her. West quietly retrieved his tape recorder.

"Ten fifty-two," he whispered into the machine. "Nearly five minutes after reanimation. Reflexes and mind have both returned, though to what degree is as yet unknown. However," he added gleefully, "subject appears to be crying. I do *not* believe that this is simple disorientation but embarrassment at having been caught trying to strangle Daniel Cain and myself."

Oblivious to his partner's observations, Cain stepped between the girl and her father. "No, Meg, don't go near him!"

"Why? What is it?"

"He-he's not well," Cain extemporized. "Emotional trauma."

"Over us?"

Before Cain could answer, Mace strode in, his .38 drawn. He took in the room and whistled. "Dan, Ms. Halsey, you all right? What the hell happened here?"

"I can explain, sir," West said, slipping the recorder into his back pocket.

"Who are you?"

"West," he said, walking toward Cain. "Herbert West. And that," he said slowly, deferentially, his eyes on the handgun, "that is Dean Halsey."

Mace's brow knit, and he studied the disheveled figure. "Dean Halsey? What the hell's he doin' under the sink?"

"Resting, sir." West wrapped his arm around Cain's, sending chills down the young man's spine. His touch was cold, impersonal. "You see, I came down here to visit Mr. Cain, who was here working. Halsey arrived moments later, and-well, he just started ranting

116

at us, sir, rather irrationally."

"No!" Megan screamed. "He wasn't irrational, just angry."

Mace looked from Halsey to his daughter. "Woman, he may have been angry *before*, but he sure looks irrational *now*."

Megan began to sob. "Daddy, no-" she muttered, and started toward him. Cain held her back, and she beat at him with her fists.

"Megan, you can't help him."

"How do you know? Let me go. I want to *hold* him!"

Cain glanced at West, who nodded; reluctantly, the young man let her go, watching closely as Megan knelt beside the Dean, her arm around his shoulders. He continued to shake and whimper like a dog, but he didn't harm her. Cain was relieved to see that, unlike their last subject, at least some of his human sensibility had returned.

Mace looked around and waved his gun at John Doe. "What's that there?"

West rubbed his hands together. "That, sir - that's a corpse."

The guard frowned. "No shit, Doc. I know it's a corpse, but what I *want* to know is what the hell it's doin' on the floor!"

"Well, we... uh... needed it for protection."

"You *what*?"

"You see, Halsey came in and grabbed that implement" - he pointed to the bone saw - "and went crazy. Daniel and I are alive only because we were able to shield ourselves with... with the body we were studying."

Mace stroked his chin, then stepped toward Halsey. "Dean Halsey? Can you understand me?"

The Dean continued to simper, his shoulders

heaving pitifully.

"Dean Halsey, just answer me - is that true?"

Halsey turned and snarled. Megan shot Mace an imploring look. He backed away. "I'm calling the police."

West cleared his throat. "Do you think that's wise, sir? There may be a scandal-"

Mace studied the smaller man. "What's with you, boy, you got shit for brains?" The guard didn't elaborate, merely bit down on his cigar and stepped around West to the wall phone. West swallowed his anger, pursed his lips, and pushed his glasses up by the bridge. Spotting the vial of reagent, he casually walked over and reclaimed it, slipping it into his shirt.

Taking in the panorama of pain and destruction, and finally feeling the bruises and cuts he'd sustained, Cain suddenly dropped to his hands and knees. Shivering and trying desperately not to heave, he shut his eyes and rolled onto his side, holding his belly.

Pulling a sheet from the doorway of the morgue, West went over and gently covered his colleague. He stooped and gave the back of Cain's hand a reassuring pat.

"It's shock, Daniel, that's all. Don't worry, you'll recover."

Cain nodded limply, and West remained at his side more to impress Mace than to help Cain.

Peering across the room, West watched the rudimentary way in which Dean Halsey interacted with his daughter. The reanimated Dean rocked against her, occasionally slobbering blood on her blouse. Halsey's inability to speak clearly suggested that, even at just over one minute, they'd waited too long to administer the reagent. But, as unfortunate as that was, West took enormous pride in the fact that at least they'd done better than they had with the savage John Doe.

And, he reflected, one thing more was also true: they'd do even better next time.

Chapter 9

The police car hopped violently as it turned off Kadath Street and hit the hospital ramp. In the back seat, Vinnie Papa listed to one side and scowled.

"He's dead, Karlin. He isn't going anywhere. Slow down."

Officer Dave Karlin acknowledged the order and touched the brake as he corkscrewed down the winding ramp. He pouted as they pulled to the curb at the basement. It was his first assignment, and not only did he have to drive slowly, but he couldn't use the siren because this was a hospital. Worst of all, it wasn't even a robbery in progress or a murder. Someone had cut up a corpse. They could have finished their Big Macs instead of tossing them aside and coming over when they got the call.

His homburg pulled low on his head, Papa stepped from the car and walked briskly toward the doors. They parted sideways, his large white raincoat swirling around him as he marched down the hall. A small, thin man, Papa had a confident step, that of a man who had the law on his side and a .22 strapped to his chest. He dealt mostly with drugs that came through Arkham on the Springfield-to-Boston run, but traffic was light since the gubernatorial election was nigh and the pushers wanted their man, "Blind Eye" Stevens, to win. So Papa was playing free safety, taking the crimes that didn't fall clearly under anyone else's jurisdiction.

He passed the elevators and shook his head as he saw a man pacing nervously outside the autopsy room. If Mace was anxious, it must've been bad.

"How's it going, Mace?"

"You know me, Vincenzo. I don't complain."

Papa knew it, all right. Mace hadn't complained when he spent three years in prison for taking mob money to throw a Super Bowl, and he didn't complain when he spent another eighteen months behind bars for beating up the mobster who'd ratted on him. Mace had been hired three years before, and quickly, when the black man who held the post before him was fired. Papa was glad to see he was still gainfully employed.

"So? What've we got here?"

Mace brought him up to date as he unlocked the door and showed him into the autopsy room. Papa took in the carnage dispassionately while Karlin deposited some undigested pickle and special sauce in a nearby wastebasket.

Papa turned to Mace. "First I want to see Halsey, then you can take me to these hotshot students." He jerked his head to one side as he started toward the door. "After that, you can show Officer Karlin here to the emergency room."

Cain and West sat on a bench in the small white cubicle on level L. In the twenty years since Miskatonic had been built, the room had been used mostly for relatives of patients who became violent, usually against the doctors who had been caring for a family member. Only once had it been used for a criminal interrogation, when the body was stolen from the morgue. Hands folded in his lap, knees bobbing, Cain was unhappy to be number two.

West sat hunched against the wall, his arms crossed tightly near his shoulders.

What had happened made no sense. In terms of cell death, the time that had elapsed between Halsey's demise and his reanimation had been insignificant. Certainly he should have come back with much more intelligence than he did... more than John Doe, at any rate. Of course, now that he thought of it, Rufus's cells did seem more settled and responsive to stimuli under the microscope; he wondered if the serum might work better in cumulative doses. Perhaps, like building an immunity to any drug or poison, the body needed time to recognize and accept the reagent.

"They're going to put us away," Cain said despondently.

West heard voices in the hall. "You're tired, Daniel, you're not thinking clearly. Just let me do the talking, and we'll be fine."

Cain snickered. "I'm going to be like Mace, working as a security guard after blowing a promising career."

West hushed him with a slashing motion of his hand. He tilted his head to the door, listening. Someone was talking about them - the level L guard, Jan Kelleher; No, Kelleher was saying, they hadn't given anyone any trouble. No, Mace said, they were not troublemakers. Yes, Mace remarked, West was strange... but Cain was not. No, he didn't think they were gay. At least not Cain. The doorknob turned, and West shot back against the wall.

"So," said Papa, studying the young men's files as he entered, "we have a pair of guys in trouble with the Dean. Then all of a sudden the Dean loses his marbles." He shut the door and looked down at the young men. "You Cain?" He eyed the taller youth.

Cain nodded.

"Cain, Dr. Hill tells me you're a good student. How'd you manage to get your loan kyboshed?"

Cain cleared his throat, choked anyway. "Sir, it had nothing to do with school. Dean Halsey wasn't happy that I was seeing his daughter, so he took it out on me that way."

"Really pissed you off, didn't it?"

"Yes sir, it did." Realizing he'd just incriminated himself, Cain added quickly, "But Megan - Ms. Halsey - and I had worked something out. If she couldn't persuade him to reinstate the loan, she was going to take out a personal loan and lend me the money. I'd have been able to stay."

Papa scratched his brow, lifted the brim of his hat.

"Presumably, Dean Halsey wouldn't have known she was doing this."

"No, sir."

"And if he found out, he'd have been furious."

"Yes, sir," Cain agreed, "but - what are you saying? That I attacked him?"

"You said it, not me."

"Great. I thought we were just talking here."

West contributed in a sing-song voice, "Whatever happened to Miranda?"

Papa leaned on the armrest, his face hard. "Miranda got out of jail on a technicality, West. But that doesn't happen here in Arkham. Guilty people go to jail, and they stay there."

West looked down at his fingernails. "I'm glad to hear that. I shall feel safe walking the streets at night."

Papa stiffened. He folded a stick of gum into his mouth, bent close again. "Dr. Hill was right, West. You *are* a cocky little shit. What about you? Some kind of vivisection you did got you tossed out of school-"

"It wasn't vivisection. It was a purely chemical experiment."

"Halsey wrote that you were cutting up a live cat. That sounds like vivisection to me. I'll bet that Dean Halsey was pretty well pissed at you, too, where he found you downstairs."

"Quite. Maybe that's what caused his mind to snap."

"That's your professional evaluation?" Papa taunted.

"It is. Check with any reputable psychiatrist, Detective. You'll find that in many people extreme stress can cause violent mental as well as physical reactions, from incontinence to madness. Given the momentary loss of awareness he seemed to suffer first, I wouldn't be surprised if the entire episode were triggered by a petit mal seizure."

"Is that a fact?"

Papa rose and faced the door as he rubbed his forehead.

"Will that be all?" West asked.

Cain shot him a stunned look, which West parried with an intense look of his own. It told Cain to back off, he knew what he was doing. Cain slumped against the wall.

Papa turned. "You two live together, right?" Cain nodded.

"Anything fishy going on?"

"Fishy?" Cain asked.

"Sexual. You guys lovers?"

Cain snickered, and West's eyes fell to the floor.

"No," Cain replied, "we're not lovers. I'm engaged to be married, for Christ's sake."

"So are half the guys who give Tootsie Pops to

125

little boys in schoolyards." Papa slipped the file under his arm. "Yeah, you can go. But you can't leave Arkham. Dr. Hill is examining Dr. Halsey right now. If there's anything in his system, like drugs that aren't supposed to be there, you guys are going to have some hardball questions to answer." He leveled his gaze at West. "Drugs, West, like lysergic acid diethylamido - say, 350 micrograms. Or JB-336. Something a smart guy like you would know how to administer, and in just the right dose to cause someone's mind to snap."

West was unintimidated. He rose slowly. "Detective, Dr. Hill stole research from a man I admired very much. I despise him for his failings as a scientist and as a human being. I assure you, if I were going to risk prison to destroy someone, it would not have been Dean Halsey."

Papa seemed pleased. "Is that a threat?"

"No, merely an observation. I believe in telling the truth, Detective And the truth is, neither Daniel nor I lifted a finger against Dean Halsey."

The detective considered this, then reached for the doorknob. "Like I said, don't go taking any trips. I may want to talk to you again."

Cain nodded, and West just stared as the detective left the room. Mace looked up from Jan Kelleher, quickly erasing all traces of the seductive look he'd been wearing. Giving the young men a low thumbs up behind his back, he went with Papa to reclaim Officer Karlin.

Megan stood in Dr. Hill's office, staring into the small padded room adjoining. Beyond the window, his face nearly as pale as his white straitjacket, Dean Halsey alternately strutted like a cock and rammed the cushioned wall like a bull. His hair stood out like tumbleweed, and there was a feverish look in his eyes, something less than lunacy but far from normal. His strength, when they'd tried to jacket him, had been extraordinary. He'd neither rested nor spoken in the hour since they'd brought him here, though at least he'd stopped spitting up blood. Only a trickle crept from his nostrils now and then, or where he broke the skin when he struck the glass.

"Daddy... Daddy, come back to me."

Hill stepped quietly behind her and laid his hands on her shoulders. "He can't hear you... or see you. That's a one-way mirror."

Her lower lip shook as her father ran to the window and made a succession of twisted expressions.

"What's wrong with him?" she wept. "Will he ever be well?"

"Until I examine him and we know exactly what happened, there's no way to determine his course of recovery."

Megan said bitterly, "It's West. Everything was fine until *he* came to Arkham."

"Unfortunately, my dear, there's nothing more we can do with our friend Mr. West. I've just been talking with President Felman. The expulsion will hold, but the university will not press charges. Felman wants this matter out of the newspapers long before the spring, lest new applications be affected. That's why I *need* you, Megan." He pressed closer. "I need you to sign a release so that I can perform exploratory surgery."

"Is that absolutely necessary, Dr. Hill?"

The lanky surgeon turned Megan around. "It is. I know how difficult this must be for you, but we can't treat what we don't understand. Regardless of the cause, I'm convinced your father's problem is neurological. And if I can find a cause, it's conceivable that I can also find a cure."

She looked up into Hill's eyes. For as long as

she'd known him, those eyes had always seemed strong to her, so wise and understanding - like Mr. Spock, she'd always thought. Now they were also soft and paternal, and she very much wanted to trust him.

"This cure," she said. "It won't include a... a lobotomy."

Hill smiled warmly. "Of course not. I want my colleague back, too, Megan - the way he was." The smile broadened. "You must trust me. We'll take every precaution."

The young woman sat down slowly in a leather armchair while Hill perched himself on the edge of his desk, his arm resting on an alabaster bust of a skinless human head. Megan snatched a tissue from his desk; dabbing her eyes, she reluctantly gave her assent.

"Good," said Dr. Hill. "I want to take a look at the right frontal lobe." He pointed to a spot on the bust. "I'll open the skull here, and if there's any-"

"Please." Megan held up her hand. "I... don't want to know."

Hill was surprised. "You've studied with me. You're not squeamish."

"He's my father, Dr. Hill."

"Precisely. I thought you'd want to understand what was involved."

"No," she said quietly. "Just help him."

He bowed once and then handed her a clipboard containing the release. Megan signed, after which she walked around the room. She paused by a framed picture of her father taken at the previous year's commencement. He looked so elegant in his cap and gown, standing proudly behind the podium. She forced herself to look at the one-way mirror. Somewhere inside that wild figure was the same distinguished man; somehow they must reach him.

"Please, Doctor," she said urgently, "let me

talk to him."

"I'm afraid that would be unwise."

"But I may be able to get through to him."

"Unlikely," he said. "And what if he were to harm you in his delirium?"

She looked with disbelief at her father. "The way he's tied up?"

"He still has teeth and a rather tough skull. And he can kick. Besides," Hill pointed out, "think of *him*, Megan. Imagine how he'd feel, recovering and learning that he'd hurt his loving, beautiful daughter."

"He didn't hurt me in the autopsy room."

"He hadn't been straitjacketed for an hour. That… changes a man."

Megan's eyes became dark slits. "Dr. Hill, you're patronizing me."

"To the contrary," he said effusively. "I'm trying to protect you." The surgeon put his arm around her. "Megan, dear, I must insist that you leave his treatment up to me," - he walked her from the padded cubicle, toward the sofa - "I want you to think of me as someone you can come to with all your problems. Or even if you're just lonely. What with your father's condition and Mr. Cain's involvement in this unfortunate matter, I know you're all by yourself now."

Megan was confused, and before she could collect her thoughts the couple was pulled around by a loud rap on the one-way mirror. They turned just in time to see Dean Halsey bat his forehead against the glass a second time, and then a third. Breaking from Hill, Megan went to the glass and shouted for her father to stop. Dean Halsey did so, backing away and staring with amazement at the mirror.

"He listened to me!" she exclaimed. "He *does* know who I am." Megan faced Hill, her expression resolute. "Doctor, I appreciate your willingness to help,

129

but there isn't going to *be* any surgery. I'm going to take care of Daddy myself."

"I'm sorry," he said sternly, "but I'm afraid I can't release him to you."

"In that case, I'll take care of him here. I'll sleep on the sofa if I have to."

Megan went to the cubicle window. "Do you hear that, Daddy? I'm going to help you!" Inside, Halsey cocked his head from side to side, listening. "I'm also going to find out what happened today, even if I have to wring Herbert West's wormy little neck to do it!"

So saying, Megan Halsey grabbed her coat and shoulder bag and hurried from Hill's office. Angrily slapping the mirror, the surgeon went to his desk and locked the medical release safely inside. Then, with a disdainful glance at Halsey, he phoned for a pair of orderlies to come and help him ready his patient for surgery.

Megan stopped at the Nocturnal Diggers Diner, ignoring the noise and activity of the upscale crowd while she sipped espresso and pondered her next move. Almost certainly she would need to hire a nurse so that her father could return to the house. She would give up classes, and, her relationship with Cain on hold - perhaps permanently, she had to admit- there would be plenty of time for her father. It was ironic, she thought. What her father had been unable to do in health he had accomplished in sickness. Even if she had time again for Dan, she wasn't sure she'd want to see him again. Whatever had happened back at the hospital, he'd had a hand in causing her father's condition. He knew her father, and he was nearly a doctor; he should have sensed something coming on. And realizing that, he should have backed off.

It was some kind of intellectual macho, she

reasoned. Her father had the upper hand at every turn but this one; Dan had obviously decided to stand his ground. She should have been flattered, she told herself, but she wasn't. The gentleness she'd always loved in Cain had been tainted forever.

Wiping away tears with a paper napkin, Megan paid the check and drove home. As she rode slowly down Wengler Street in Arkham's old-money North Side, she thought of how lonely the large stone home would be without either her father or Dan. Whenever her father was away, she stayed with Cain or he was there; there had never been a time when she wasn't busy trying to repay one for all he'd done for her or please the other and ease his workload. Now she had a helpless man to take care of, and while that would occupy her she knew it could never fulfill her, not in the same way. She pulled into the driveway and wept with her head on the wheel.

"Dan, what have you done to everything?"

She wanted to go back a day, run away with Dan, and prevent all of this from happening. Satisfying both men as best she could had seemed so important just a few hours before. Now nothing mattered. She didn't know how she would live without her father, without Dan.

Megan didn't remember leaving the car. She went through motions mechanically, suddenly aware that she was standing in the large foyer. It didn't matter how loudly her keys jangled; her father wasn't asleep. She shucked off her coat, her bag dragging on the floor as she walked to the staircase. Where were the sounds she was used to hearing whenever she came home - professors laughing, Hill pontificating, her father settling an argument of some kind?

"Hello, Megan."

The young woman spun toward the living

room. "Daniel?" She peered into the darkness as Cain rose and switched on the light. His expression was dour, repentant, but she felt no pity; gazing at him, she despised him even more than she hated West. "Get out."

"Megan, I know how you feel, but we have to talk."

Part of her wanted to run at him and smack him; another part of her wanted to be held. She looked away and started up the stairs.

"Megan, please-"

"What more is left to say?"

"Things," he said mysteriously.

Megan stopped. "What... *things?*"

"Facts," he mumbled, "things we dared not tell the police. I tried to tell your father this afternoon, but he wouldn't listen. You saw too... the cat."

Her eyes were hard, her voice even harder. "What does the cat have to do with Daddy?" Megan started back down, and Cain's eyes lowered to the hardwood floor. "Daniel, what did you and West do to him?" Cain turned away, and the woman stormed over, grabbing the front of his jacket and pulling him around. "Dammit, what happened? What did you and West do to him to make him like that?"

"It was horrible," he admitted, his voice cracking. "I didn't mean to - that is, I didn't want to hurt him."

Megan slapped him hard. "What did you *do* to him? Why is my father insane?"

"That's just it. He-he's not what you think."

Megan slapped him again. "What are you *talking* about? Even Dr. Hill doesn't know what-"

"There's a lot Dr. Hill doesn't know. Your fa-ther's not insane, Megan. He's... dead."

The young woman froze. Her head turned

slightly with disbelief, and then rage consumed her completely. She launched herself at his chest, both fists flailing.

"Liar! *You're* insane! *You're* the one who should be locked up!"

"Megan-"

Cain tried to hold her, but she pushed him back and continued punching at him.

"Get away! I wish you were dead!"

"I didn't mean to hurt him," he said at last. "Or you. You know me, Megan. I'd have died rather than do that."

Her rage turned suddenly to confusion, and, sobbing heavily, Megan slid toward the floor. Cain caught her, easing her down. She struggled briefly to get away, but he clutched her close to him, whispering that he would tell her everything and work with West until they found a way to cure her father. Burying her face in his chest, Megan wept out her shock and sorrow, finally returning his embrace. Her arms stung the cuts he'd suffered battling the two bodies that night, but to Cain it was the sweetest sensation he'd ever felt.

After a few minutes, Megan quieted and then dozed off. It was more than an hour later, nearly three A.M., before she awoke. Curled against Cain on the living-room floor, she insisted that he explain exactly what had happened in the morgue.

His explanation was straightforward, but no less incredible. Megan sobbed repeatedly during the narrative, though she didn't doubt a word of it. The transfer papers from Zurich had glossed over the details of West's research, but they were explicit about his genius. And she had seen enough medical miracles at the hospital to accept one more, even one of this magnitude.

At Cain's prompting, Megan then told him

what had happened after he'd left. When she mentioned that her father was incarcerated in Hill's office, he swore.

"Dr. Hill examined your father?"

"Yes. He even wanted to do exploratory surgery on him."

"Shit. If he examined him, then he probably found the reagent in his system." Cain rubbed his eyes, which were tired from the long day and having watched over Megan while she slept. "It's too late to do anything about that now," he reflected, "but just don't let him do any cutting. If he gets a look at that saturated brain tissue, we're all cooked."

"He won't," she assured him. "I signed a release, but he knows I don't want the surgery done."

Cain shot her a look. "You what?"

"I signed a medical release. But that shouldn't matter. Dr. Hill would never go against my wishes."

Cain was on his feet. "Like hell he wouldn't. The man's a scientist!"

"Daniel, you're overreacting. He may be a little stuffy, but he's not irresponsible."

"Don't you see?" he persisted. "Never mind that you've given a very curious scientist a very unusual brain *and* permission to examine it. If your father doesn't recover, what ambitious neurosurgeon stands the best chance of being named the next Dean?"

"He wouldn't dare! I'd fight him."

"And lose, badly. He could always claim your father became violent and had to be put under the knife. You wouldn't stand a chance against his word *and* the signed release. You know those papers protect the hospital against everything."

Megan still wasn't convinced that Hill would betray her, but she also wasn't willing to take any chances. Leading the way to the car, she broke several laws en route to the hospital and several more once they reached the building. Using her father's key to enter through a side door, they climbed the stairs to level C. There, outside Hill's darkened office, Megan took a moment to brace herself.

"You all right?"

She nodded, then used the master key to admit them.

The room was cold, and they kept their jackets on. Megan hurried to the cubicle, Cain went to the filing cabinet. Jimmying it with a letter opener, the young man began flipping through the file of medical releases while Megan stared at her father through the one-way mirror. Dean Halsey was lying in a corner, unmoving, his face to the wall. His hair was brushed back and his straitjacket clean; he looked like a polar bear, big and innocent, and Megan ached to hold him.

"How is he?" Cain asked.

"Sleeping, thank God."

Seeing that Cain was engrossed in the files, Megan went to the cubicle door and, opening it, tiptoed to her father's side.

Across the room, Cain saw and heard nothing. He'd found a file with Megan's name on it and pulled it out, expecting to find the permission document; instead, what he saw made his legs grow weak. Inside were artifacts - not just photographs of Megan going as far back as her high school graduation, but also a tightly knotted lock of her hair, a microcassette labeled "Megan poetry recital," and various notes and letters written in her hand.

"Jesus," he muttered as he went through the thick stack of material. There were postcards, ticket stubs, dinner checks, newspaper clippings from her days as a cheerleader, and even a soiled napkin.

"Megan, you'd better take a look at this. I think

we've got a problem."

When the young woman didn't answer, Cain looked up.

"Megan?"

There was a scream from the padded room, and, spotting the open door, he ran over. Swinging through, he saw the young woman holding her hands to her cheeks and gazing down at her father. There was a dumb expression on Dean Halsey's face, and his head had been shaved to the middle. In the middle of his forehead was a large white bandage.

Cain's spirits plummeted. "Oh, Christ."

Moving Megan aside, he gently pulled up a corner of the bandage and studied the wound. Dean Halsey neither made a fuss nor acknowledged Cain's presence in any way.

"Dan, what has Hill done to him?"

Cain didn't answer. He simply examined the sutured hole and, after a long moment, replaced the bandage.

Rubbing the back of his neck as he rose, Cain said, "It looks like a laser drill."

"Which means?"

"It means we're too late," he said gravely. "I'm afraid your father's been lobotomized."

Daniel Cain would remember Megan's long, terrible scream for the rest of his life. And as he stood there trying desperately to calm the hysterical woman, he vowed one thing above all, somehow he would make Dr. Carl Hill remember it, too.

Chapter 10

"Rufus, bless you - you're worth more than all the bodies in China."

West was hunched over the microscope, intently watching cells scraped from Cain's cat. The cells were alive but oscillating violently.

"Reagent applied to brain tissue of thrice-dead cat," he said, scribbling frantically in his notebook. "There's apparently no limit to how often tissue can be reanimated, but the trauma increases geometrically with each application." He laid his pen aside and scratched his chin. At once frustrating and intriguing was the drumming on the roof from a sudden downpour. He would have to ask Cain if Rufus had been afraid of the rain in life, if the cells themselves were shaking in part from some form of racial memory.

"Regardless" - he continued writing as he spoke - "there must be some kind of analgesic which won't upset the reagent and can restore stability without suppressing natural functions. Or should I be looking in the other direction, exciting it to a degree where it has the power to control itself?"

"I'd try the latter," said a sonorous voice from atop the basement steps. West spun and saw a vague figure standing in the dark hallway. "After all, it works on hyperactive children; it should work on a mere cell."

"Who's there?" West demanded, twisting the desk lamp toward the door. The cone of light revealed a dark, wet trench coat topped by the craggy features of Dr. Carl Hill. His face looked tired, and there was the hint of grayish stubble about his hollow cheeks. But his eyes were elated. West frowned. "What do *you* want?"

"I think you know the answer to that, Mr. West." West braced himself, said nothing. "I want to know why Halsey's heart fibrillates-"

"I don't have to talk to you."

"Why his pulse is erratic-"

"I told everything I know to the police."

"Why he cries out in pain-"

West stood, his expression petulant. "You can *leave* now, Doctor!"

Hill came forward, dragging his finger idly down the long table. "I want to know why he does all of this, Mr. West, when we both know that he is quite... dead."

West nervously adjusted his eyeglasses and turned his head away.

Hill bent the light into the room and looked around. "Hmm... interesting little laboratory you have here." His eyes settled on the microscope, and he wiggled a scolding finger. "Ah, Mr. West, I recognize this - no doubt taken without the proper requisitions. But then, a young genius like you has no time for formalities. You had your eye on this microscope, on our chemicals and... more perishable supplies when you were back in Zurich. You didn't come here to study, did you? You came to use the best-equipped labs in the most out-of-the-way school you could find. You came, in short, to be anonymous."

"Yes, I came to be alone. Take your microscope and get out."

Hill grinned. "Surely you don't think I came for that?"

"Then what do you want?"

The surgeon rubbed his hands together. "First, to satisfy my curiosity. Were you sent here, Mr. West?"

"What?"

"Did someone give you a mission to plague me?"

West waved an index finger at the surgeon. "You're being paranoid, Dr. Hill. Plaguing you was entirely my own idea."

"In that case, to what end?"

"To protest what you are - a thief."

Hill seemed saddened. "Then it *is* you, Mr. West. It's not Willett or the Josephs or blind devotion to Gruber. This foolish hate... is yours."

"Just as my research is mine, which is a boast you cannot make."

The sadness became tinged with anger. He had to fight to keep it down; "You're being petty, Mr. West. I'd hoped that if you were carrying someone else's banner I could reason with you to lay it down, convince you to do your research under my auspices."

"And have you steal from me as you stole from Professor Gruber? I was not born yesterday, Doctor."

"Nor were you born wise, it seems. I can offer you my resources and complete privacy. You can accomplish twice as much as you are now."

"I'm afraid you miss the point."

"And *I'm* afraid!" - Hill's rage got the best of him - "that you miss *my* point, Mr. West. One way or the other I will have your discovery... whatever it is that gives the dead the appearance of life."

West's shoulders came back. Despite the accusations and insults, it was this which finally offended him.

"It is not the *appearance* of life, it *is* life. This is not magic!"

"Can you prove that?"

"If you need proof of my reagent's power, put it on your next hamburger instead of catsup. The results will astonish you."

Hill's anger abated, the scientist once more in control. "Mere movement is not life. Halsey would not take food, and he battered himself without pain trying to reach Megan."

"Which proves my point. He was responding to his daughter. The formula interprets and then recreates, exactly, each cell. What comes back to life is the subject as it was at the moment of death. Miss Halsey was on her father's mind when he died, so she is on his mind now. Just as, if he were hungry before dying, Halsey would now take nourishment. Or if he'd been carnally aroused, his foremost priority would have been sexual in nature. I grant you, these are imperfect creatures, but they are not mere automatons. They are alive!" He added dryly, "As you say; *I* am a scientist."

The insult did not go unnoticed. Hill's mouth grew rigid. "I'll have you locked up for a madman... or a murderer. You will do what I tell you to do!"

"I think not."

Hill circled around West, his eyes burning, holding those of the young scientist. "To the contrary. Did you know, Mr. West, that before going to Switzerland I spent time in many other countries? And in India I met a man who taught me how to focus the mind to achieve any goal, physical or mental. That was what sent me on my quest for the will and the soul in the cerebral cortex." West's eyelids began to droop. "You see, Mr. West, by speeding up respiration and slowing all other movement, I can actually nourish that area in specific to boost my intellectual capacities briefly... to solve a problem... to operate with greater dexterity at a crucial moment... to force you to do what I bid." Wavering where he stood, West took his notebook from the desk and handed it to Hill. Hill smiled. "You see, Mr. West? You may control the dead, but I can control the living. Soon I shall control both."

The surgeon broke his stare, and West put his hand to his brow. Hill laid the book beneath the lamp and began to read. As he did so, his mouth widened.

"I see. Good God, I see. It *is* life!"

He turned the pages more rapidly, his finger leading his eyes down the center of each. "Genius, Mr. West! Your extension of that old fool Gruber's work is really quite... brilliant!" He snapped the book shut and picked up a small vial of reagent. After studying it for a moment, he gestured toward the microscope. "Let us see my new serum at work, shall we?"

At once furious and impressed with what Hill had done, West thought feverishly while he did what he was told. He remembered the cat carcass, burying it in the yard that morning. He smiled to himself as he slipped a fresh slide into the microscope and used tweezers to take a new specimen of tissue from a soap dish marked "Arcane," a disguised form of "Rufus Cain," used to keep from upsetting his roommate.

"Dead cat tissue," he announced, urging Hill to the binocular eyepiece as he picked up an eyedropper. "The reagent," West said, applying the formula and backing slowly away.

Hill's face exploded with delight. "Magnificent!" West continued to step away, feeling behind him. "This is miraculous!"

The youth felt the shovel's stiff handle and wrapped his fingers around it.

"Yes, Mr. West. Yes! I will be famous!"

West brought the shovel around hard, flush against the side of Hill's head. There was a loud snap, and Hill fell writhing to the floor.

"Yes," West agreed, "you will be famous. But not for stealing my reagent!" He straddled Hill's chest and stared into his pinched face. Lifting the shovel, he brought the blade down on his neck. Hill's eyes went wide, as blood poured freely from both sides of the wound and from his mouth. Mechanically, West raised the spade and brought it down again. This time he reached to the backbone; the third time he severed it completely. The head lolled to the side, stopping when the nose wedged against the floor; blood from the neck continued to wash over it like a fountain.

"There's one problem laid to rest," West remarked as he watched Hill's hands and feet twitch for several seconds after decapitation. When they were still, he stood staring at the head for a long moment. Suddenly, he dashed over and, grabbing a handful of the surgeon's blood-streaked hair, picked up the head. He plunked it into a dissecting pan, and the head rolled over; he righted it, but once again the head dropped to its side. Finally, West grabbed a memo spike from the desk and, setting it in the center of the tray, impaled the head upright.

"Stay, damn you," he muttered as he sought the reagent. Filling the hypodermic, he jotted the amount in his notebook. "Parts... whole parts. I've done the brain, but never whole body parts."

Injecting the head at the base of the skull, he hurried to the body. Squatting in the thick stream of blood still pumping from the neck, he emptied the remainder of the dose into the heart.

Sitting back on the stool, West tapped the pencil impatiently on Hill's head while he waited. He checked his watch. Ten seconds, eleven, twelve. The eyelids fluttered. Scribbling down the time, West looked back at the body. Nothing had happened. He looked back at the head, the glassy eyes now fully open.

"Wessssst!"

The voice was a sibilant, airy whisper, the cheeks filling and blowing puffs of air past the lips. West was astonished. Hill's urge to speak transcended even the loss of his lungs and voicebox. He'd only been dead a half-minute; time did make all the difference in the world.

"Yes, Doctor, it's Herbert West. What are you thinking?"

"Wessssst…"

"Yes?!"

"Wesssst… yoooou… bassssstaaardd."

The youth frowned. "Never mind that now! I take back what I said, you *are* a scientist! Now *help* me. What are your sensations, what are you feeling?"

Hill's nostrils oozed blood into his trembling lips. "Come… cloooooser."

West readily obliged, and Hill's glazed eyes rolled slowly to the left.

"Yes… what is it? Speak!"

Hill continued to stare as a pair of powerful hands clutched West's head and drove his forehead hard into the table; with a small moan, the young man fell unconscious.

Something like a laugh slipped from between Hill's pale lips as the body edged from behind West and gently removed its own head from the spike.

"Feeeels… bettttter… " Hill cooed, looking up at his own torso. There was a large clot atop the neck and glistening streams of blood down the front and arms of his overcoat. He felt all of the sensations the body experienced, yet he still felt oddly superior to it;

143

proof, he thought, that the soul was indeed located entirely in the brain.

The body carefully cuddled him under its arm, from which vantage point Hill surveyed the room. He instructed his ambulatory half to collect the notebook and vials of reagent in the refrigerator, all of which were crammed hastily into the coat's deep pockets.

"Go..." Hill said, looking toward the door, and the reanimated body obeyed, walking stiffly from the house and staying to the shadows just beyond the street-lamps.

Hill was delighted to find that he could direct the body's every movement simply by thought, from changes in direction to using a sleeve to blot away the water splashed in its eye by a passing motorist. Though they shared no physical sensations, they shared that bond; and when they turned the corner and the wind knifed off the nearby Concord River, the body went so far as to hold the head close to keep it warm. Hill was touched by the gesture and could not help but wonder: if he decapitated other bodies and destroyed the heads, could he build an army of devoted slaves?

He would try it very soon. First, however, there was other business to which he must attend.

When he was a child, West once balanced volumes A through F of the *World Book* on his forehead. He did it to counteract the stiff neck he suffered from hours bent the other way, peering into his microscope. He awoke now feeling worse than he had then, with enormous pressure on his brow and a deadness in his ears, as if they were stuffed with cotton.

However, nothing compared with the sick horror he felt when he looked up and saw the empty dissecting pan. His glasses slipped off his nose, and he quickly rammed them back on. There was no doubt about it, the head was gone. He spun: so was Hill's body. He looked to the left: so was the formula. He spun to the right: the refrigerator door was open, and the formula was gone from there as well. He rose on weak knees and staggered back, knocking over the stool.

"My work!"

There were footfalls upstairs, and West staggered over, falling against the banister.

"Hill? Hill, is that you, you son of a bitch?"

He started up, stopping when Cain appeared in the doorway.

"Daniel!" he wheezed. "My work! He took my work!"

"Who did?"

West backed down the steps, bumped into the refrigerator. He threw his hand toward it. "Hill. He took my serum, too, except for what I have upstairs. He took my serum... my notes. Everything!"

Cain hurried down. "Herbert, you're insane! What really happened?"

West clutched at Cain's jacket. "He's alive!"

"Hill? No kidding, and he's been *very* busy tonight."

"No, you don't understand. I had to kill him."

Cain grew rigid. "When?"

West looked at his watch. "About an hour ago. But he's not dead anymore."

Cain understood then, and shook his roommate violently. "Damn you, Herbert. This isn't a goddamned science project - it's murder! This has got to stop!"

"Daniel, you still don't understand. He tried to blackmail me!"

"That doesn't mean you had to-"

"And he wanted you to disappear!" he lied. "This is a conspiracy, Daniel. He's trying to do with us

145

what he did with Gruber."

Cain released his companion and took a step back, almost losing his balance in the pool of blood. He looked at it, then at West. "You brought him back to life and he left? With all his faculties?"

"He did. The miserable bastard is *perfect*. Well, almost perfect. He suffered a rather... disfiguring wound. His mind" - West jabbed at his own - "that, Daniel, is just as devious as it ever was. The serum works!"

Cain nodded with understanding. "A conspiracy," he repeated. "Of course. That's why he did it."

"Did what?"

"Operated on Dean Halsey. He lobotomized him so he could control him in case he ever tried to talk or tell somebody what happened."

West slammed the refrigerator door shut. "So he could protect *his* discovery. Very clever."

Cain splashed through the blood to the steps. "Yes. I've got to tell Meg."

"What does Meg have to do with this?"

Cain paused. He pitied West just then, less for what he'd done to Halsey and Hill than for the transparent resentment - or was it jealousy? - that he felt toward Meg. But he needed West's help and explained, "Hill's got this weird file on her, full of napkins and hair and photographs. I think he's projected some sort of psychotic need onto her."

West arched his brows comically as he tried to imagine Hill proposing to her, down on one knee, his head between his feet.

"I wouldn't worry about Dr. Hill losing his head over her," he said, laughing. "It's too late!"

The laugh grew until Cain began to doubt West's sanity. The night had taken its toll overtly and also in insidious ways; perhaps the fragile fence West had always straddled had been undermined, pitching him headlong into madness. He would see to him later. Right now, Megan was his concern. With the Dean out of the way, he only hoped Hill's compulsion was not among the qualities restored by West's formula.

The lumbering body opened the door to Hill's office and walked in, crashing into the bookcase, bouncing off, overturning a standing lamp, and pinballing into the filing cabinet before finally reaching the desk. There it felt around for a dissecting pan, one Hill had left there after the Halsey surgery. Finding it, the groping hands pushed away the small section of brain tissue and rested Hill's head on the paraffin.

Its eyes shut, mouth sagging, the head sighed. The wax was softer than the cold tin in West's lab, and it felt so good against the raw flesh of the neck. But he was tired, much too tired to open his eyes; he urged the body to hurry with the serum.

Fumbling in its pockets, the hands withdrew a vial and the hypodermic, clumsily stabbing its finger while trying to find the stopper. Finally filling the needle, it injected the head with a fresh dose. Hill rationalized that whatever hadn't been absorbed by the brain had dripped out the neck; he made sure the needle went higher this time, almost vertically along the medulla oblongata and up the wall of the braincase.

The serum worked almost at once. Hill felt the tingle of renewed vigor in his surviving senses, and his mind quickly regained its edge. But there was still a haze behind his eyes, and he suspected the reason for that. Ordering the body to inject itself again, he sent it off to a refrigerator beside the cubicle.

The body clipped the edge of the desk and caused the head to slide to its side. "Caaaareful...

oooaf!" Hill scowled as, disoriented, he was unable to prevent the body from stumbling into the armchair. Righting itself, it groped for the refrigerator, spilling a shelf of croquet trophies beside it. Pulling open the door, it returned with a plastic pouch of blood. Unscrewing the cap, the body squirted it into the tin.

"Yeeessss..." Hill moaned as his hungry tissue soaked up the blood: When the pouch was empty, the body obediently followed Hill's silent commands to pick it up - though by the hair, not the neck. The ragged edge was sore from having rubbed repeatedly against the overcoat sleeve on the way over. The body turned the head around slowly until its eyes came to rest on the cubicle. Smiling, Hill ordered that he be carried over.

"Alllaaan!" he suspired when his face was near the glass. "Allaan!"

Halsey stood, his dumb expression showing signs of comprehension. Still straitjacketed, he shuffled over, falling to his knees by the mirror. He pressed his face to the glass, saw Hill's face beyond. He grunted in recognition.

Hill opened his mouth to speak, but blood oozed from the corners, obscuring his speech; he'd taken too much, wouldn't be so greedy next time. Using his tongue to push out the rest, he said, "Allaan! I want you... to come ouuut... noooow."

Obediently, Halsey staggered to the door, where the body met him and released the latch.

Hill instructed the hands to raise him so he was eye to eye with his servant. Then, his eyes wide and bloodshot from the infusion, he patiently and meticulously explained what he wanted Halsey to do.

Chapter 11

Cain drove the side of his fist against the six panel door.

"Megan! Meg, are you there?"

He heard the sound of her slippers on the floor. "Dan?"

"Yeah. Are you okay?"

She flicked the deadbolt and opened the door. "Sure. Why?"

He stepped in and hugged her. "Nothing, Meg. I was just so afraid!"

"Dan, what is it? You're shaking."

"I don't know, I was just... worried about you."

She wriggled free, once again demanding to know why.

Cain shut the door and said evasively, "I just feel horribly about everything. I guess I'm getting paranoid." He looked into her eyes. "It's just... it'd be so hard to lose you."

Megan pulled her robe tighter and wrapped her arms around her waist. "I think you should know, Dan, I tried to hate you. I wanted so very much to hate you."

"I'm glad you failed."

She looked at him. "I still love you, and I always will. But I've been thinking - in spite of that, you should go away; Transfer to another school, get away from the doubts and the stares. You need some time alone to think about all of this, and I need to think about what to do with Daddy and Dr. Hill."

Cain smiled. "Then let me help you. Y'know, it's funny. I came here to suggest that you get away, go and live your life. Find somebody. But when I try to imagine being somewhere or doing something without you, I know that what I'll want to do is drop-"

The splintering of the door drowned out the rest of Cain's words. The couple jumped reflexively as a pale fist came through, followed by another. The fingers splayed, and the arms withdrew, pulling the door with them; arms flailing, Allan Halsey stepped through the huge hole.

"Daddy!"

Before he knew what was happening, Cain was in Halsey's grip, being pressed against the wall. Halsey dispatched him with a hard blow against the old plaster, then dropped Cain to the floor and turned on his daughter.

"No, Daddy!"

The zombie chased her into the darkened living room, exhibiting no trace of familiarity with her or his surroundings. There was only single-minded purpose in his wild eyes. When she bumped up against the piano and pleaded with him, he simply scooped her into his arms and headed for the door. When she screamed, he grabbed a lace coverlet from the arm of a chair and stuffed it violently into her mouth. She continued to struggle, and he swung her head hard against the brick of the fireplace. Megan went limp, and, with a snort of satisfaction, her father left the way he'd entered.

Lenny Wengler panted hard as he jogged down Wengler Street. The young attorney did it every day, rain or sun; his great-great-great-grandfather had built this section of town, and it filled him with satisfaction to run each morning past the old trees Isaac Wengler had planted with his own hands, the stately mansions he'd built, the rental properties he himself owned up and down the street. He liked to make sure everyone was keeping his homes neat, the grounds manicured, the facades clean. It was a heavy responsibility being a landlord in a town where appearances were important, and tradition, austerity, dignity, and pride were expected to be upheld at all costs. He noticed a tag-sale sign on a tree and ripped it off without ever missing a step; he wadded it tightly and dropped it into a sewer grating as he crossed the street.

Wengler breathed deeply as the sun rose over the river. There was something awe-inspiring about the sunrise and money contemplated in tandem. One allowed him to enjoy the other fully, and he smiled as he savored the sweet new day.

As he always did, he ran toward the Halsey home, hoping to catch a glimpse of Megan leaving for her morning run. If anything could improve on the beautiful harmony of daybreak and money, it was the sight of the young woman in her shorts and T-shirt breathing heavily as she ran down the road. Glancing toward the house, he saw something he couldn't quite understand: Dean Halsey carrying his daughter in his arms; Halsey looked as if he'd fallen out of bed and down a flight of stairs. Sucking down a deep breath, Wengler hurried over.

"Allan, what happened? Is Megan all right?"

Thoughts of mouth-to-mouth resuscitation pranced through his head as he saw that Megan was unconscious. He hoped there hadn't been an explosion; his most expensive home was right next door.

"What's wrong? Can I do anything?"

Halsey continued walking, oblivious to Wengler's approach. Wengler came around by Halsey's side, saw his face and whistled.

"You look beat. Here, let me take her!" he said. He slipped his arms under Megan's shoulders. "I'll run her to the hospital."

Halsey growled and tried to pull her away. Wengler reached for her again.

"Say, old boy, don't be ridiculous! You're in shock, and your daughter needs-"

Halsey jumped forward and locked his teeth on Wengler's nose. The young man squealed as the zombie snapped it off and moved down to his throat. With Megan still in his arms, he held on to Wengler's suntanned flesh, oblivious to the young man's cries and the pounding of his fists. Jerking his head back, he ripped away most of the attorney's windpipe. Wengler's eyes rolled back into his head, and he dropped, blood pumping energetically from the wound.

Spitting out the nose and throat tissue, Halsey stepped over the body and continued on his way. Another early-rising jogger, engrossed in her Walkman, saw the zombie and his daughter and just shook her head. It was, she decided, one of the more transparent hazing gags that she'd seen in recent years.

Dressed in his green surgical attire and carrying a medical bag, Dr. Hill strode boldly from the elevator and down the corridor toward the morgue. Perched on his shoulders was the head from his desk; hidden behind a mask and cap, it had not drawn undue attention from the few people he met. Hill's real head was in the bag, held upright by surgical sponges stuffed on the sides.

It had been an unusually long ride from his office.

Since the head couldn't see, it had had the body press each floor to be sure and get the right one. The head had simply counted the "dings" as they descended and ordered the body out when they reached the basement.

Because the plaster head was held on with a carefully concealed neck brace, Hill's body was able to move quickly down the hall. It breezed past Mace's desk. The guard barely looked up from a copy of *Boudoir*.

"Is that you, Dr. Hill?"

From inside the medical bag, the head said in muffled tones, "Yesss... it's meee."

"Gonna be here for a while?"

"Yessss."

"Can't hear ya through the mask, Doc–"

"*I - said - yesss,*" he repeated distinctly.

Mace nodded with approval, then returned to the magazine, switching his cigar from side to side while Hill fumbled for his key. Finally opening the door, Hill accidentally brushed his head against the doorframe as he entered, and one of his fake ears fell off; he left it, hoping Mace hadn't heard. Listening just inside the autopsy room, Hill was delighted when the guard got up and left, mumbling about finally having time to bop his baloney.

"Sexual... deviant," he muttered as the bag was placed on the operating table. Hill squinted as the top was unzipped, the white light pouring in. But the fresh air was welcomed, and he gulped it down; as he did so, he raised a stream of bubbles in the pool of blood which surrounded the base of his neck. "Thaaaat's... better," he gasped, then looked around.

153

The room looked different from this height, bigger and more important. He felt like a child again, awed and invigorated by life; it impressed him almost as much as his own power over death.

"Piiick... me... up," he ordered, and his body did so, again by the hair. When he was facing the morgue, he asked to be put down and then ably directed the body toward the morgue. It returned wheeling a cadaver. Hill was pleased at how good he was getting at this and reflected that it was not unlike driving a car - albeit one whose alignment was crude and response slightly delayed. He wondered how far he could be from the body and still control it and whether he'd be able to manage two at the same time.

"In... goooood... time," he told himself.

After all, he had eternity.

The body's heavy footsteps thudded loudly in the large room as it went about its chores. First it shut and bolted the double doors. Then it moved the head onto a small stainless-steel instrument table and rolled the corpse to one side of it. The operating table itself had to be free - for later, Hill thought giddily. Finally, the body retrieved the laser drill from its hook at the head of the instrument table.

The corpse was that of an old man, in his eighties.

He would have been relatively tame at the end of his life and thus ideal, Hill had decided, as the second member of his army of lobotomized slaves.

It was, he thought, the dawn of a new age of intelligence. The next step in evolution, the unimind - not just an almighty ruler, but a single intelligence who would be a part of every human. He would put West to work finding a way to link his mind with other bodies, and then he would become like God himself, a part of all, supervising the research of Herbert West in one city, making love to a woman in another, all the while taking an energizing blood bath. And his enemies, the scientists who had crossed him or hated him - he would make a museum of their still - living heads and visit them daily, taunting them with his power and achievements. Especially Gruber. He'd have his rotted head dug up and reanimated. Perhaps he would pack them into satellites and send them into space, with enough serum to keep them alive for a lonely eternity. Or shrink them, in the manner of headhunters, still alive, feeling every moment of torment.

He wondered if he could also become a cheetah, racing at lightning speeds after a gazelle, or a hawk chasing a prairie dog, or a shark prowling the seas... with heads of his enemies bobbing about. And what about the long dead, like Edison or Michelangelo? Could he bring them back, too? Put them to work creating new wonders for his amusement?

And the stars. To a man who could live forever, traveling to the farthest reaches of the universe was hardly a problem. He could visit other worlds, conquer them, use their science to become even more powerful.

Then there was the greatest mystery of all. He remembered nothing from the brief period when he was dead, but with the proper recording devices could he die again and come back with a complete awareness of everything that had transpired?

The possibilities were endless. He could conquer, he could be resurrected. He could make a miniseries of his life and force everyone to watch. And applaud. And watch again. The calendar would start from the year 1 C.H., and on his birthday he'd find a way to make the sun itself shine more brightly!

The body tapped him lightly on his head. He came around, the sound of crowds cheering giving way to the low hum of the laser drill generator. Hill shut his eyes.

"Soooon... soooon," he told himself. First he must build the house before he could live in it.

West walked briskly up Wengler Street, his eyes on the ground. The concrete was old, and the roots of neighboring trees had split it here and there. Despite all he knew, he still marveled at the phenomenon. It was what had started him on his career-as a child, staring at the walks in Toronto, wanting to know how what appeared to be frail and perishable could bend cement to its will. Learning about how new cells replaced old ones over time, like soldiers being sent to the front, eventually putting enough pressure on the obstacle to break it.

His parents had sent him to a psychiatrist because, while other children played soccer, he sat on the lawn and talked to the street. They didn't understand that he was talking out the things he'd read in science texts, thinking aloud in order to proceed to the next logical step. The last time he'd talked to his parents, they still didn't understand. He wondered if the fire had been simple to comprehend. It had been child's play. Literally.

He didn't need them or anyone now, except Cain. He was the only one who could help him - stop that lunatic Carl Hill.

He felt the sole vial of reagent in the pocket of his black overcoat. They would triumph. They'd pin all of this lunacy on Hill and be hailed as heroes; there was nothing the college wouldn't give him then, and he'd be able to continue his research unbothered. It wouldn't matter, then, what Cain did. He liked the young man and enjoyed being with him, but he was not a true scientist. He would make a fine general practitioner and husband.

West checked the numbers of the houses. When he reached 775, he hurried up the long, curving walk and rang the bell. In the early-morning light, he noticed that no weeds had cracked the walk at Dean Halsey's home; they'd all been cut down. He smirked, but the smile vanished when he saw the broken door. He hurried up the front steps into the foyer.

"Daniel!"

He dropped beside the body and felt for a pulse. "Thank God. Daniel!" He slapped both sides of his face. "Come on, wake up!" Cain moaned, winced. "Dan, what happened?"

Cain felt the back of his head. "Dean Halsey-"

"He did this?" West looked quickly at the wound. "A contusion, maybe a mild concussion. You'll be all right."

Cain started. "Meg! Oh my God."

"What happened?"

Cain pressed his palm to his forehead. "Halsey - strong, like that other body. He came through the door, but that's all I remember."

"Hill must have sent him for Megan," West reported. "I don't think there's anyone here now."

"Where then, Herbert?"

"At the hospital, I'd imagine." He rose, hands on his hips. "Can you stand up?"

Cain pushed off the floor, and the room went black; he fell back against the wall. West started toward him, but Cain held up his hand.

"No - I'm fine, let's go."

The two walked hurriedly toward Miskatonic, whose white walls shone in the rising sun. The chrome of the marquee glistened red like fire; if hell had a marquee, Cain told himself, it would look like that. And if hell had a master, he would certainly resemble Dr. Carl Hill. After all he'd done these past few days, Cain was convinced that he'd learn soon enough about hell firsthand.

Hill's body shifted the pan around so the head had a clear view of the surgery.

"Fiiiine... begiiin."

The gloved hands flicked on the instrument. The red beam sizzled to life, and the body put the drill to the old man's forehead. Smoke rose from the pale flesh, and an acrid smell filled the room, like burning rubber. Although he didn't need to breathe, the fine smoke stung his eyes; he had never before appreciated how valuable were such simple things as being able to avert one's head or wipe one's eyes. Bloody tears formed, leaving tracks down the side of his nose.

There was a knock on the exit to the rear of the room. Hill looked back too quickly, and his head did a slow pirouette on the bloody paraffin. He was able to steady himself by tensing his neck and ear muscles, and regained his balance.

"Goooo" he said impatiently to his ambulatory half.

The body obediently hung the drill on its clip and made for the double doors in front.

Hill rolled his eyes. "Noooo... stupiiid. The... baaack... dooooor!"

The body stopped. Its shoulders drooped, and it seemed hurt. But it turned and walked stoutly toward the rear of the autopsy room, where it threw the huge bolt and opened the metal door.

Hill's face brightened when he saw Halsey in the doorway, the robed Megan unconscious in his arms.

"Gooooood... Enterrrr..."

Halsey toddled along, a strip of Wengler's flesh still lodged in the side of his mouth. Hill was glad to see Halsey had obviously shown some initiative, though he hoped he hadn't been followed; he needed a bit more time to finish his preparations.

The zombie placed Megan on the operating table, her head inches from that of Hill. The surgeon's eyes were saucers, the skin of his face tight with expectation.

"Oh... yeeeessss... "

Halsey was standing several paces back, staring at the ceiling. Hill looked over and caught the zombie's attention; he jerked his eyes toward the young woman, and Halsey came forward obediently.

"Take... the robe... offff."

Halsey grabbed a fistful of fabric and stepped back. The robe tore away, and he discarded it.

Hill ran his eyes along her naked form. "Tie... herrrr!" he commanded. "Sheee... must... not... leeeave..."

His body came over and began binding her to the table, tying the straps tightly around her wrists and ankles. Hill stretched his neck, rose up an inch.

"Sooo... lovely... " he leered. "You... will... keeeep ... your... heeead."

Hill had his body pull off its rubber gloves and sent it, with uncharacteristic grace and reverence, to Megan's side. Its hands moved to her breasts, gently cupping and caressing them, now and then squeezing harder as his passion rose. Hill shut his eyes, savoring every moment. She was sweet and wholesome to the touch, not like the rough women he was used to buying in Springfield or Boston. He moved one hand lower, to her flat belly. His thumb and index finger were callused from the months of pressing so hard on the laser drill. The skin was thick and dead, which frustrated him; he had to lay his open palm on her to feel her softness completely, her warm belly thrilling him as it rose and fell beneath his hand.

Megan stirred. Her head rocked slowly from

side to side, and her eyes fluttered open. Hill felt a single tremor shoot through her.

In the first moments of wakefulness, she still couldn't place where she was or what she was seeing.

The head beside her was huge and grotesque, like a Halloween mask. Its eyes were shut, but there were streams of dried blood along the cheeks and caked in the tangled hair. The tongue, visible in the wide open mouth, was swollen and reddish-purple; there was bloody spittle around it, and a foul, tart odor rose from within. It was the scent of death, and it overpowered even the sour smell of burning rubber which seemed to hang in the air.

Megan looked down. She felt the hands on her, saw what they were doing; then she saw where she was. With a mounting sense of horror, she looked to the right and saw her father standing idly by. Suddenly it all came back to her, what her father had done, and her fears escaped in a single gut-wrenching scream.

Hill's eyes popped open. Megan saw them and shrieked again, simultaneously trying to rise. Finding that she was lashed to the table, she tugged violently against the straps; one of the leather pieces slipped from its metal tooth, and her left arm flew free. It struck Hill's body, which went sprawling back against the instrument table. The hit was a solid one, too great for the neck brace, and the plaster head toppled off, shattering on the tiles. Gaping at the huge clot, from which fresh blood was percolating, Megan's throat went raw, her wrists and ankles bloody as she tore to get free.

Hill rasped something like a laugh and ordered the body to pick him up. It did so under the ears, tilting him so he could stare into Megan's face.

"I've alwaaaays admired... your beeeauty, my dear."

The young woman shut her eyes and cried piteously.

Hill's brow arched softly. "I think... I've alwaaaays... loved you."

"No! *No!!*"

"Yesss... it's truuue..." he said as he had his hands moved his head to the side. He put his discolored tongue into her ear, and she screamed again, pushing at his forehead with her free hand. But Hill's hands were stronger, and he only smiled.

"You will... looove me!" he said as his hands pulled him lower, to her chest. The fat tongue came out and encircled one breast, then the other. He looked up at her again. "You *will!*"

Megan arched her back, tried to push him away. "Please stop! Let me go!"

"That's it... my dearest... Meg. More... passion! I've always... imagined you... a passionate looover!"

Hill's tongue trailed down her chest to her navel. Talking was becoming easier as he mastered it, and he could clearly feel his body responding to what he was seeing and tasting. West had missed something important, that each subsequent dose of formula restored more of the original being. He was for all intents and purposes whole - and then some.

Megan twisted to her side. "Daddy, please help me!"

Halsey jumped slightly but continued to stare blankly into the room.

"Yooour... father cannot help. He… is mine… just as you… willlll… be mine." Hill's tongue slid down further.

"No! What are you doing to me? God, *no-no!*"

Poised above Megan's crotch, the head looked up at her and smiled. "Yes... my love! *Yes!*"

With a twisted smile, he watched her quiver

helplessly beneath him, then opened his mouth wide and disappeared between her legs.

Chapter 12

The air was sweet and cool despite the rusty smell which rose from the corpse. Detective Vinnie Papa was pacing on the sloping lawn behind the body, wondering where the other car was, while photographer Valerie Burk took pictures. It was early, and there were only two other teams on duty; still, one of them should have been here by now. Or maybe he was just being impatient. No one had been slain in Arkham for six years, and there hadn't been an unsolved murder in more than twenty-five years. Bad enough one record had fallen; he was not about to lose the other one.

When Burk had finished, she motioned Officer Karlin over from the curb. He pocketed the handkerchief with which he stood wiping his mouth, then took a folded sheet from the trunk of the squad car. He used it to cover the victim's body, then returned to the curb.

"You shouldn't eat till you learn to control that," Papa said as he marched to and fro.

Papa hated wimpy cops; he would give Karlin a backbone if it was the last thing he did. More than gutlessness, though, he hated waiting. He was a man of action, but he didn't want to start knocking on doors until reinforcements arrived. The last thing he needed was for Karlin to get sick again and fail to stop a passerby from stepping on the soft mud which had washed from the lawn during the last rain. There was the faint outline of a footprint in the mud, and it didn't belong to the woman jogger who'd found the body.

Something clicked in Detective Papa's head when he saw the two young men round the corner. He watched as they stopped, looked, and then headed the other way down the street. He ceased his pacing and sent Karlin to collect them; he smiled with self-satisfaction as Daniel Cain and Herbert West were escorted over.

"I thought it was you."

"And you were right," said West. "Now, may we go?"

The young man snatched a look at the sheet. There was blood in the area of the face and throat. Teeth had obviously been used against the victim, not hands. The hands must have been full...

Papa glowered down at the youth. "A bit uppity this morning, aren't we?"

"We're in a bit of a rush this morning."

The detective took a deep breath. "A bit early for a class -"

"It's an experiment in progress," West said. "We can't afford to be late."

"I see. Sure, you can go - just as soon as I ask you a few things."

He motioned to Karlin, who looked away as he lifted the sheet.

"You know this guy?"

Cain looked down then away. "It's Len Wengler. He owns half the town."

"Probably has a lot of enemies," West offered.

Papa eyed West. "Probably. On the other hand, you guys have this weird knack for showing up whenever there's trouble. I mean, you were there when the Dean went fruity and carved up a corpse, and here you are again, minutes after someone had his face chewed off near the Dean's house. Is it just that you're lucky, or is something going on I don't know about?"

West locked his hands behind his back. "As you know, we are friends of Dean Halsey's daughter. It's hardly a coincidence that we are in the neighborhood."

"*Both* of you... at this hour?"

"Daniel's alarm didn't go off. I came to get him."

"And didn't see the body?"

"I came down Hecate Lane. Unless the victim was maimed there and then jogged here, determined to get in that last block before dying, how could I see him?"

Papa pushed out his lower lip. "If that's the case, why did you head the other way when you saw me here?"

"To avoid precisely the kind of delay we're experiencing." West made a point of pulling back his coat sleeve and tapping his watch. "Detective, we really do have an important experiment going on at the school, and if we're late several months of work will go down the drain."

Papa looked from West to Cain. "Is that so? You look nervous, kid. Anything wrong?"

"No, sir!"

"You had more color up at level L." West said, "He hasn't slept since then."

"I'm talking to *him.*"

West stared hotly down the street, the toe of his shoe doing an angry dance on the pavement. Though Cain towered over Papa by more than a head, at the moment he seemed the smaller of the two men.

"So, Cain? What gives?"

Cain took a deep breath and said quietly, "The truth is, sir, I may have AIDS. That's what we're going to the hospital to find out." He looked down at his feet. "And if you must know, that's why Dean Halsey was so upset."

Papa took a step back. At that moment, West saw in his face everything he hated about the human race: fear, prejudice, self-absorption, and ignorance. He could see that, unlike most doctors, he would have to administer his serum very selectively. Certain people just didn't deserve immortality.

The detective's mouth curled wryly. "So I was right about you, huh?" Cain said nothing. His voice tinged with superiority, he said, "You're queer, and you bullshitted me. Let's hope that's all you lied about. Yeah, get out of here, but I'm warning you. If you happen to be anywhere near another crime, you're both going to jail - sick or not."

Papa resumed his pacing, and the young men continued on their way. When they were out of earshot, West said, "That was very clever. I'm proud of you, Daniel."

"Christ, I hated to lie like that, but I was thinking about Megan."

"As well you should."

"Jesus, what's going to happen when Papa goes to the house? He's going to see the smashed door and come after us."

"Let him come. *We* didn't break the door, *or* kidnap Miss Halsey. Her father did that, under the direct orders of that ogre Hill. Let the detective question him and then dare to cast aspersions on *us!*"

His face twisting with apprehension, Cain began to jog. West fought to keep up with him, his hard-soled shoes clip-clopping as he ran.

They reached the hospital within minutes,

West breathing hard as they made their way through the main lobby to the elevators.

"Where to, Herbert? Office or morgue?"

"The morgue. I've got a feeling that abducting Miss Halsey isn't the only mischief he has in mind for this morning."

They waited for an elevator, but Cain grew impatient and hurried to the steps. He feared the worst when he emerged in the basement and saw that Mace was not at his post.

"He might have killed him." West read his mind. "Mace would make one hell of a powerful reanimate."

Walking cautiously to the door, they listened for a moment. All was quiet within, and slowly, gently, Cain tried the knob. It was locked. He pointed to Mace's desk, and West went over. He retrieved a key from the top drawer and handed it to Cain. His heart driving hard against his throat, Cain slowly opened the door. West snuck through the opening.

Circling the room, he was more amused than repulsed by what he saw.

"I hope I'm not intruding."

"Eh?"

Hill's reply was muffled, his vision blocked. He immediately ordered the hands to raise him. Gore from his neck dripped down the insides of Megan's thighs. She had to bite her lip to keep from shrieking.

Hill's mouth turned up at the edges.

"Missster... Wessssst! An unexpected... surprise!"

West shook his head. "I must say, Dr. Hill, I'm very disappointed in you. You steal the secret of life and death, and here you are trysting with a bubble-headed coed. You're not even a second-rate scientist."

"Weee... are... in love!"

Megan screamed in protest and slapped violently at the head with her free hand. The body moved out of reach. It held the head close, waist-high, like a huge, ugly tumor.

"She has... much to learn... as... do... you!"

"At *your* side? I doubt it." West paced a moment, weighed his words. Without being obvious, he looked past the head toward the door. Cain was creeping gingerly toward Megan. West wanted to buy him time to get Megan out, to make Hill jealous, irrational. Careless. "I doubt very much there's anything you could teach me," he went on, "save for a better way to lie and deceive."

The head smiled. "You... flatter... me. The truth... Mister... West... is that I am... actually glaaaad... to see you!"

"Why? Run up against a problem you can't solve?"

The head cocked a brow in Megan's direction. "I doubt... Mister West... whether that was something... of which you have... any... knowledge."

West slid his hands into his pockets, his gaze wavering. He took the insult, concentrated on the larger goal.

"No," the head continued, "I am... glaaaad... to see you... because it saves me the trouble... of haaaaving to... send for you!"

"And why, I wonder, would you have sent for me? To kill me?" West felt for the hypodermic in his pocket and took a few steps closer to the head. "To pump me of anything else I might know?"

"Arrogant... fool! I am... finished... with you!"

"That's what you think." West saw that Cain had reached the table and was undoing the straps. "You'll never get credit for my discovery. Who's going to believe a talking head?"

Hill's head puffed to the best of its ability. "Seeing... *is*... believing!"

"Only at the circus, Dr. Hill, and I suggest you get a job there, in a sideshow. That's all you're good for now."

The head sunk in its hands. "I have had... enough. Though I am... puzzled. Tell me... why an intelligent young man... like yourself... should make such a foolish, fatal mistake... of coming here... to challenge me."

West rocked on his heels, encouraged as Cain finished freeing Megan and handed her her robe. "Oh… I have a plan."

Hill had his hand pluck a hair from his mouth. He grinned. "Do you? Well..." His voice was unusually flip. "So... do... *I!*"

It wasn't until the dead had risen that West even noticed them. The corpses had been wheeled from the morgue and left casually about, in the shadows beyond the surgical spotlight, where no one was likely to see. Now a half-dozen body bags burst in unison, their occupants surging in different directions.

In a single, sweeping glance, West recognized each of them. Meatball. Burn Victim. Cracked Rib. Shotgun Wound to the Head. Hill had reanimated them all. Even Rotten came to life, her arm hanging by a few tendons, her neck and breasts half eaten.

Then Malpractice awoke and bellowed at Hill, confirming West's suspicions. But the zombie quickly remembered its programming and snarled at West. The young scientist watched with amazement. How was Hill controlling them? What power did he have to suppress and activate the reagent-and all at once?

It was only when Shotgun Wound to the Head passed under the bright surgical spotlight on his way to the door that he understood. Amidst the creature's other wounds was a small fresh hole just beyond the hairline. The corpses had been lobotomized by the laser drill. One - Cracked Rib - had also been decapitated, no doubt a prelude to a more advanced form of control. Hill may not have had much scientific know-how, but there was nothing wrong with his imagination. He was an entrepreneur.

Still facing West as his zombies spread slowly through the room, Hill craned around his own waist and yelled, "I know... you're back there... Missster Cain... and so... do they!"

Cain said frantically, "Hill, stop this madness!"

"Why... Missster Cain? So... *yooooou*... can have... sweet... Megan?"

When the zombies were positioned along every wall and corner of the room, Hill laughed heartily, blood trickling from his mouth.

"Taaake... them!" he gasped. "Clooose... the... circle... and kill them!"

Wailing like banshees, the zombies rushed forward. Cain and Megan dove under the stationary operating table, but Meatball easily wrenched it from the floor and tossed it aside. The couple scurried toward the exit where Halsey stood.

West needed a diversion. "Mace!" he yelled, his cry turning Hill toward the door. There was no one there, but it gave the young scientist the instant he needed to duck from a pair of closing zombies and withdraw his hypodermic. Arm cocked, he charged Hill's back.

"Foooool!" Hill sneered as one hand hoisted his head onto the stump of his neck, staring straight back, while the other locked around West's wrist. "Did you think... I would fall... for thaaaat?"

"You *bastard!*"

West clenched his teeth as Hill's powerful fingers crushed his forearm. His hand went numb, and he released the hypodermic; with a disdainful flick of the wrist, Hill tossed him into the arms of two waiting zombies.

"Ahhhh... my impetuous friend... you will sing... a different tune... verrrry soooon!"

Behind him, Hill heard the sounds of scuffling feet. He shut his eyes and looked through Cracked Rib's head, which sat on an overturned bucket in the sink. He had injected some of his own brain cells into Cracked Rib's skull along with the serum; it was his mind which had been duplicated in the dead man's brain. The image was blurry, but he could see Cain and Megan in the clutches of his army. He watched as the reanimated John Doe reached for Megan's face, his fingers bent like claws. The young woman screamed. The joy of their recapture, of his ability to see through the eyes of another, thrilled him.

Hill shouted suddenly, "Enough!" The zombies went still but didn't relax. Their prisoners were held firm. Only two of the six slaves, those holding West, were at all uneasy: Malpractice, who was shifting slowly from foot to foot, blood pouring from his mouth as he snarled at Hill; and Meatball, who used one hand to fish around in its mouth and reel out its tongue. He snapped it off and tossed it aside, happier once he was able to release a full-bodied roar without the impedance. A dark look from Hill silenced him and caused Malpractice to fall still.

Hill ordered the zombies to bring West to the operating table. He had his body place his head back in the bloody pan while the zombies forced West onto his belly, facing their master.

Hill smiled. "I will show you... power... Missster West."

171

The hands squirted in more blood, and he paused, moaning contentedly. A dreamy expression came over him, and Hill once again regarded his prisoner.

"My discovery... the laser surgical drill... makes possible... a new technique... in lobotomy! It results... in total mastery... of the human... brain." He threw a manic look around the room. "These... reanimated subjects... have proved to be... a successful test. They... and more like them... will give me power... undreamed of... *power*."

"You corrupt man!" West charged. "Look at these creatures! You've created stupid mutes. That isn't why the formula was invented!"

"Spinoffs," Hill replied.

"No! Gruber and I wanted to end suffering, not cause it This is *wrong!*"

"Don't... talk to me... of virtue... Missster West. You. wanted... the world... to laud you... and Gruber. I... have taken... the liberty of... deifying myself!"

Cain shouted, "You're no god, Hill, you're a devil! You're dirt!"

Hill inched his head around on the slick paraffin. "Verrry... powerful... dirt," he corrected.

Ordering his body to activate the drill, he signaled Malpractice and Meatball to flip West around.

"No... wait! What are you doing?"

"Helping you... to see... the light!"

Hill's hands brought the instrument over, focusing the slender beam just above West's right eye.

"Oh, God! *God, no,* not my brain! *Please leave me my brain!*"

"But I will... Missster West. Only... under my... controllll."

West began whining and kicking violently

172

against the table, and Hill ordered Halsey over to hold his feet. Waking with a start, the Dean shambled over, past Megan.

"Daddy, listen to me! It's Megan-Megan!" Halsey stopped before her.

"Halseeeey... over... *heeeere!*"

The Dean started away.

"Daddy - look at me!"

He stopped again, and Hill, impatient, ordered Cracked Rib to put his hand over her mouth. The zombie did so. Halsey stared at his daughter's struggles.

Hill had to bellow to be heard over West's screams.

"Halllssseeey…"

Cain sensed his indecision. "Dean Halsey, *help* her! It's Megan, your daughter - your *baby!*"

Halsey snorted, studied her.

"Silence... him!" Hill yelled. John Doe reached around to shut Cain's mouth. As he did so, the young man wrenched his arm free, simultaneously stomping hard on the cadaver's foot and pushing back. The foot tore away, and John Doe fell helplessly to the ground. Cracked Rib, headless, did not see Cain's fist coming; he punched the zombie in the side, sending it flying toward Hill. Shotgun Blast released Megan and turned on Cain. The young man grabbed Megan's arm and yanked her back.

"Get behind me!"

Much to Cain's surprise, Halsey suddenly joined Shotgun Blast in the attack.

"Wait, Dan, he thinks you're hurting me! Daddy, I'm all right! Get Dr. Hill!"

Halsey paid her no attention, grabbing Cain around the throat while Shotgun Blast locked an elbow around his forehead. The right side of his face missing,

Shotgun Blast had to keep his head twisted awkwardly around to watch as he worked to crack Cain's skull like a nutshell. Jumping at him, Megan put both hands to his face and pushed; the neck snapped, his head falling limply behind him. Stunned, he turned on Megan.

"Dan!"

Desperate, Cain drove his knee into Halsey's stomach. His grip weakened momentarily, long enough for Cain to tear his hands away. Diving to the side, he threw his arms around Shotgun Blast, trying to pull him away from Megan.

"Hill, damn you, he'll kill her!"

"Then I... will give her... life!"

Halsey regrouped, began pulling at Cain. "Daddy, not *him* - *this* one!"

To help the Dean, Cain decided to let go and back away; as soon as he did so, Halsey began tearing at the back of the zombie who was molesting his daughter.

Across the room, Hill watched the tide of battle with mounting displeasure. Sending his body into the morgue with the serum, he shook with elation as it returned with reinforcements. Though he had not had time to lobotomize them, he believed the zombies would join in whatever activity involved their fellows; he was right. The four newcomers, newly dead and not as pasty-pale as the others, fanned out through the room, a petite Slit Wrist girl and brawny One-Armed man hastening to hold West down, while a tall, skinny corpse and a bald operating room victim lurched toward the lovers.

Cain watched the proceedings with mounting horror. As soon as Halsey had succeeded in freeing his daughter, Cain pulled her behind a stainless-steel table which he used to keep the others at bay.

"Daddy, get Dr. Hill!" Megan yelled. "Get the

head!"

With a growl, Halsey charged through the room, heaving tables left and right. His attack was met by Hill's body, the two locking arms, each pushing hard to bring the other to his knees.

"Killlll... " Hill screeched. "Killlll... killll them all!"

Obediently, One-Arm released his hold on West's arm and went for his throat; Slit Wrist did likewise. His hands free, West scooped up the laser drill which was hanging beside the table. He shone it into the male zombie's eye, driving him back, then turned on the girl, blinding her in the near eye. She too retreated, and West rolled off the table.

Hill raged, "Nooo! You... must... stop him!" Instead of obeying, Slit Wrist and One-Arm stormed around the room, lashing out blindly. They tore at shelves and cabinets, smashing mindlessly until, spotting the other zombies gathered around Megan and Cain, they hastened to join them. Megan swatted fiercely in every direction.

"Daddy, help us!"

Halsey turned, blood oozing from his lower jaw, which he'd lost in the battle with Hill. Hill's body seized the moment to latch onto him by the shoulders. He flung him to one side, but Halsey grabbed Hill as he fell away, and the two of them went crashing through the double doors into the hallway.

They spilled over Mace's desk, smashing the phone onto the floor and knocking over the large fluorescent lamp. It sparked and died. Watching from a dark corner, where he'd gone to try and spot the reagent, West was actually glad to see something die and stay dead.

Halsey and Hill climbed to their feet and, running together, fought back toward the autopsy room.

Sauntering back to his desk, the copy of *Boudoir* rolled in his fist, Mace stopped and gaped.

"What the fu-?"

Tearing his eyes from Dean Halsey and the headless body, Mace didn't try to understand what he thought he saw. He simply ran for the pay phone down the hall.

Inside, as the ring of zombies closed in on them, Megan decided that their only chance lay in stopping Hill. Crouching below the table, she snuck to the side and broke for the instrument table. Cain lunged after her. "Meg, no!"

Cain was caught about the waist and neck by a pair of zombies. He saw a third zombie bolt after Megan with incredible speed.

"Meg - look out!"

Burn Victim snared her by the hair, and, seeing this, Halsey pushed Hill's body away and stormed over.

Megan fought her revulsion. She stretched her hands before her, toward the dissecting pan, and Halsey looked over. "No, Daddy, forget me! *Him!*"

At that moment, watching his former colleague, Hill was both disgusted and pleased. Pleased because he'd been right about the location and power of the soul. He hadn't touched the Dean's cerebral cortex, and Megan had obviously reached it. She'd stimulated fond memories deeply buried in Halsey's soul, and, responding, it had performed a miracle, nothing less than a cerebral bypass.

However, Hill's pleasure was extremely short-lived. That same soul obviously held not-so-fond memories of him as well, perhaps of the surgery. He could see hatred flood Halsey's being, hatred which paralyzed the surgeon, made him unable to rouse his body to action. With a wrathful cry, Halsey sprung at the defenseless head.

"Allllan... nooo!"

Halsey grabbed Hill by his ears and banged the head repeatedly against his own forehead. Throughout the room, the first batch of zombies stopped, stood, wavered. Herding creatures, the other four did likewise.

"Alllan... put... me... down!"

Halsey did - hard. He dropped the head to the tile floor and then retrieved it by its hair. Dazed, Hill was unable to summon his wits to call for his body. He tried desperately to spark activity in Cracked Rib's head, somehow transfer his mind to it, but he was too confused. His body nauseous from what was happening to the head, Hill spit up blood. Two of the zombies did likewise.

Cain rushed to Megan's side.

"It's incredible. He's tied to them, and they're all feeling it!"

They watched in stunned silence as Megan's father put the head between his palms and began to press. His fingers dug into the eyes; there was no pain, only a cry of frustration as the eyes finally popped and blood poured down the cheeks.

"Heeeelp... meee!"

Hill's cry jerked his body to animation; it felt its way forward, but not in time to save the head. Halsey cracked the skull, and, when he heard it give, he stretched both hands behind him and heaved it into the hallway. The pulped mass exploded and coated the wall with fine pieces of brain, bone, and flesh.

Mindless, Hill's body finally reached Halsey, colliding with incredible force. Halsey fell against the instrument table while, around him, the equally mindless zombies converged.

Cain clutched Megan's hand. "Come on-"

"No." She resisted. "We've got to help Daddy!"

"Megan, he's dead!"

"Not all of him!"

She started toward him, and West scooted over, blocking her way. There was a pair of hypodermics in one hand, a vial in the other. The laser hole in his head was blue and hideous, his face bruised and dirty. But he was alert as ever, his manner coolly efficient.

"Daniel's right, Miss Halsey, there's nothing more *you* can do. I'll help him."

"You've done enough!"

"Hardly. There is work to be done."

"More killing, you mean."

Cain said, "Herbert, I know you're disappointed, but, for God's sake, leave this mess for the authorities."

"Look, I told you I have a theory," West said as he filled the hypodermics. "It's the same thing that happened to Gruber."

"Overdose?" Cain asked, his interest piqued.

"Correct. Depending on how much he gave them, the others will wear off. But not Hill. I must know if it works."

Cain reached for one of the hypodermics. "Give me one. I'll-"

"You'll do nothing," West interjected, "unless one of the others interferes. In that case, there's a fire axe in the hallway. Use it to take off its head." Their eyes met, and there was a flash of mutual respect; Cain for West's dedication, West for the way Cain had adopted his own cause. Cain wished him well.

"See you outside," West replied, rising.

Megan resisted as Cain started for the door.

"No - my father!"

"Megan-"

"You *saw*, there's still something there!"

He hesitated, watching as Hill and the others tried to bring Halsey down. Before Cain could react, the corpses surprised him by showing a semblance of unity. Savage hands locked themselves around the Dean's arms and head and tore them off, hurling them away like Olympic hammers. Watching, Megan mewled and fell limp; Cain caught her and started toward the door, his eyes on West.

Pushing up his glasses, West wondered if Hill had been able to organize the attack through Cracked Rib's head. It was a fascinating notion, but he didn't have the time to consider it just then; using the distraction of Halsey's demise, he circled the mad group. When he was directly behind Hill, he ran at his back and punched the needles in hard, just below the clotted neck. The headless body jerked upright, so fast that West couldn't hold the needles; they remained in the neck, bobbing like antennae, as the body whirled on its attacker.

West easily ducked the groping hands and watched Hill. He hadn't gotten to empty the hypodermics, but that would probably have been overkill. Already the body was beginning to quake.

"Good riddance, you son of a bitch!" Cain stopped. "Herbert, come on!"

West didn't come, but went deeper into the room, looking under the tables.

"I won't leave without my notes! I can't continue without them."

"Continue! Are you *crazy?*"

West didn't answer, and Cain was distracted by Hill's body, which was now quivering wildly. Unable to keep its footing, it fell against a cabinet and slipped to a sitting position, every inch of it alive and undulating in waves beneath the robe.

Leaderless now, the other creatures resumed their rampage, tearing blindly at the tables, fixtures, and each other - the first group of zombies against the second in what Cain could only conclude was a sick clannish rivalry.

West paid the corpses no attention. Spotting the medical bag peeking from beneath a discarded body bag, he picked his way over. Cain watched with alarm as Shotgun Blast crouched, frog-like, on the other side of the up ended operating table.

"Herbert, look out!"

West spun, but not in time. The creature leaped and landed square on his back, sending him sprawling. It immediately began banging West's head on the floor.

Laying Megan down in the doorway, Cain bolted back into the room. He threw his shoulder into the zombie and bowled it over, the two of them tumbling into the morgue. Shaking his head vigorously, West continued toward the medical bag.

"Be right there!" West shouted as Cain grappled with the powerful Shotgun Wound. He grabbed the kit. "We'll OD them all!"

Through clenched teeth, Cain yelled, "Hurry!"

Reaching into the bag, West suddenly realized he didn't have a hypodermic; swearing, he made for Hill's still-convulsing form. Avoiding the monsters to the left and right, he didn't hear Malpractice stalk up from behind; the zombie took him by the shoulders and heaved him across the floor, West landing hard against the iron legs of the sink. Before he could collect his splayed wits, Malpractice and the hobbled John Doe had crossed the room and were upon him.

Cain saw what had happened but was unable

to tear himself away from Shotgun Blast. The brute had backed him to the wall and, his knee to Cain's chest, kept him pinned to the wall while he raked at his face. Though the youth was able to tear away chunks of the dead man's fingers, the bones and sinew held firm. Blood trickled from the deep gashes along Cain's cheek and nose.

With a common foe to fight, Slit Wrist came over to help Shotgun Blast. Falling to her knees, she began biting Cain's thighs, and together they brought him down. Cain's head struck the wall as he fell, and he knew in that instant that he was going to die. Dazed, he shut his eyes and tried to marshal his senses for the attack; instead of feeling teeth and nails on his throat, however, he heard a hollow "bong" and looked up.

Slit Wrist was wearing a confused look as she felt her caved-in-skull, while Shotgun Blast turned just in time to catch the bottom of the metal fire extinguisher in the undamaged side of his face. Propelled by a spray of dark red blood, he rocketed backward, Megan leering at him as he fell.

"Go to hell, you miserable bastards!"

Cain scrambled to his feet, his vision blurred and head throbbing.

"Home run," he said as he steadied himself on Megan's shoulder.

"Hurry. I smashed another one on the way in, but there are three on West."

Cain followed her out and saw that Cracked Rib had joined the fray and was fishing through the medical kit. Cain noticed the severed head then, still alive and glaring down.

"Incredible," he said through the pain and grabbed the fire extinguisher. He sprayed a jet of foam across the room, and the head dropped backward into the sink. The body ran to get it. Cain threw the fire

181

extinguisher at his shoulders and sent him sprawling. Almost immediately, he regretted it, however, as the remaining zombies came at them.

West pushed his head from beneath Malpractice's knee.

"Dan - the drill!"

Snapping his fingers once, Cain dove toward the instrument table. The laser drill was still spitting its filament of fire, and Cain grabbed it. Fumbling with the keypad on the side, he punched the beam to full power and, turning it on One-Arm, he set his clothes afire. The zombie stared aghast, then slapped at the fire as his dry skin went up like kindling. Cain pivoted to take the attack to John Doe, who had left West. As luck would have it, that was the moment one of the creatures decided to punch the fuse box through the wall. The beam died, and the lights went out.

"Shit!"

Cain swore again as one of the male zombies - in the dark, he couldn't be sure which - pressed forward and grabbed him. Megan ran up behind the creature, pounding him, but he knocked her back without even turning. Cain could smell its breath, unspeakably rank, as it tried to bite him. Remembering what had happened to Lenny Wengler - and also to Dean Halsey's fingers when he first attacked John Doe - Cain didn't try to push his face back but, instead, struck down with his elbow, clubbing the zombie over and over in the ear. The creature retreated, and Cain squirmed away, scooping up Megan. They stumbled through the morgue to the autopsy room.

Lit with two emergency lights and the fire of the burning zombie, the room was growing thick with smoke. Somewhere to the left, plumes of white suffused the darker haze as one of the zombies gleefully spilled jar after jar of acid on itself and on the countertop. Near the overturned operating table, two of the zombies were tearing at the corpse of a third.

Cain squinted through the stinging smoke. "Herbert!"

There was coughing on the right, by the sink, and they felt their way over. West lay bruised and bloodied, draped over his bag. Behind him, Hill's body was still spasming; they heard a grotesque slurping sound from within it.

Cain refused even to try and imagine what was making the noise as he helped West to his feet.

"Come on, pal, let's go."

The young scientist rose unsteadily and grabbed the bag, following the others toward the door. Suddenly, the slurping became a roar, and West reached for his throat.

Cain peered back through the smoke and felt his stomach buckle.

"Christ! *Christ!*"

Like a monstrous snake, a length of intestine had uncoiled from the surgeon's belly and grabbed West's throat. The overdose hadn't killed Hill but had given every inch of him its own hellish life.

Cain stretched around and reached for the young man, but West was jerked backward, toward Hill's body. The intestine reeled West in, wrapping tightly around his torso and legs and lifting him from the floor.

"Caaaaaain!"

"Herbert, hold on!',

Cain looked frantically for something to use against Hill. Finding nothing, he attacked with his feet. However, he was driven back by the body's reserves. The stomach sprayed acid while the other organs began exploding violently, one after the other, keeping Cain back with blinding waves of gore.

West waved him back. "My... notes!" he gurgled weakly. "Get them... out!"

Cain looked around and was about to pick up the bag when Megan began screaming. Cain spun and saw what was left of her father standing beside her, its head at its feet and staring up at her. The mouth moved.

"Meeeeeaaaaggggggaaaannnn..."

"No-no-nooooo!"

The young woman started laughing madly. Snatching up the medical kit, Cain led her away. Her laugh became a sob and then a cough as she choked on the smoke. Cain handed her a handkerchief and held his own breath. Behind them, they could hear the crack of bones as the intestines tightened around them, zombies still moved blindly about, smashing the room and each other.

Megan gagged, stumbled. "I can't... can't move."

"Don't give up now-"

"Dan... everything spinning!"

He picked her up. *"Hold your breath,* we're almost there!',

Cain wiped his eyes as he fought through the burning waves of smoke. He kept his gaze on the dim light of the hallway and, fighting unconsciousness himself, hunched over and all but fell toward the corridor. When they reached it, he lay Megan gasping on Mace's desk and dropped beside her. Noticing Hill's smashed head on the floor, he pulled her to him, making sure Megan couldn't see it.

"Everything's going to be all right/' he said into her ear. "We're safe now."

Somewhere in the distance a fire alarm sounded, joining the din of the zombies and the crackle of flames. Yet through the cacophony. Cain heard a faint, plaintive cry, a voice high and pained but clearly that of Herbert West: "Gruber, I join you.. I join you!"

It was followed by a scream and then silence.

The silence, Cain reflected, of permanent death.

Chapter 13

Cain opened his eyes. It seemed as if hours had passed, though he knew only seconds had gone by. His mouth was dry, and he struggled to swallow down the flat, smoky taste that filled it.

The shadow crept slowly along the table. Cain saw it, and, his muscles aching, he turned over slowly.

"Mace?"

He looked up at features that were not those of Mace. Burn victim.

Reacting rather than thinking, Cain pulled Megan to the floor just as the zombie dumped two beakers of acid on the desk. He shielded Megan as they fell, droplets searing his back and neck. Cain shrieked with pain. Following the sound of his cries, the surviving zombies staggered from the autopsy room. Roused by the pain, Cain jumped up and threw a block at Burn Victim. The surprised zombie fell back, and Cain helped Megan to her feet.

They ran for the elevator, Cain barely ducking in time as one of the zombies picked up Mace's wooden chair and hurled it down the hallway. He lost his footing on some of Hill's blood and fell. Megan helped him up, then slapped the elevator button, the two pacing frantically as the digital numbers clicked off above it. The initial sting of the acid had worn off on Cain's back, and now it burned horribly; he asked Megan to tear open the holes it had burned in his shirt, to keep the fabric from rubbing.

The zombies paused to smash Mace's desk and rip the telephone from the wall before continuing on. It didn't comfort Cain to know that they meant him no malice, that they were simply destructive by nature. He picked up a leg of the shattered chair, swatted it threateningly against his open palm.

"Wish this thing had a nail in it," he said.

"Why, would that stop them?"

He shook his head. "I just want to rip those sons of bitches apart."

Megan watched the indicator while Cain watched the zombies.

"It's here!"

The door slid open, and the couple jumped in, pushed the button for the main floor. Cain flung the chair leg at the zombies to dissuade them from approaching; the panel began to close and was nearly shut when a section of the desk came flying back in response to the chair leg. It wedged between the door and the return panel, the former opening obediently.

"Fuck me!" Cain roared and jumped behind the desk. He pushed; as the wood slid out, he failed to see Burn Victim reach for him, the zombie having hauled her scabbed body beside the carriage. She grabbed him by the hair and, using her own momentum, threw Cain down the corridor. Then she stepped into the elevator.

The door began to close again and the zombie began strangling Megan. Cain swore, but a powerful pair of hands grabbed him and flung him even further back. The remaining zombies turned on Cain, cornering him in the opposite end of the corridor. Thick smoke poured from the autopsy room and obscured the elevator, blocking all but Megan's smothered screams. He called to her, was prepared to run into the approaching creatures when be remembered the axe.

Cain saw it hanging on his side of the autopsy room, just behind one of the approaching creatures. With a roar which actually startled the creature, he heaved himself forward and, spinning the zombie aside, grabbed the axe without breaking his stride. He raced to the elevator, where the leg of Burn Victim herself was preventing the door from closing, and it was the first limb to go. Cain lopped it off at the knee and jumped in. The door finally shut behind him.

Falling to one knee, the zombie pulled Megan with her, her hands still locked around the young woman's neck.

"Let her *go!*"

Cain brought the blade down hard on Burn Victim's shoulder, cleanly severing her arm. The zombie made no outcry. She simply rose on one leg and turned on Cain, grabbing his throat while the amputated limb still choked Megan. Her mouth hung open, showing blackened teeth where the lips and gums had burned away; she snapped at Cain as he clawed at her with one hand. Her seared flesh came away easily, and he exposed half her jawbone and skull in a mad effort to get to her brain and stop her.

Black circles swam before his eyes, but Cain was aware of Megan falling silent and slumping against the wall. With a burst of strength, he took the axe in both hands and swung it at Burn Victim's head. Though he was pinned in the corner, Cain had put enough force into the blow to dig deeply. The zombie backed away, and Cain swung again. This time the head came off. It fell, still alive, but the shock had caused its arms to go slack. Before it could react, Cain swung the axe again, splitting the head lengthwise. Both halves fell away.

Its arm and body undirected, Burn Victim was no longer a threat. Cain pushed her aside and knelt beside Megan, felt her neck. Placing his hands on her chest, he began pressing down.

"Come on, Meg, breathe! *Breathe!*"

The elevator door slid open. From the corner of his eye he could see firefighters rushing into the lobby. There would be questions, and he had no time for them. Scooping Megan up in his arms, he punched the basement button. He stumbled over the medical kit on his way out, picked it up, and hurried toward the emergency room. The door shut behind him, carrying Burn Victim away.

Patients and hospital personnel alike looked up as Cain rushed by. He ignored them and also the firefighters as they hurried past him to the stairwell. He felt a flash of guilt for not warning them about the zombies, but Megan needed him more. And what would he tell them?

Several of the nurses and orderlies recognized Megan as Cain hurried past, and they dropped what they were doing to come along. The noisy queue snaked toward the room, and Dr. Harrod emerged to see what this latest commotion was about. When she saw who it was, she swore violently.

"Cain, what happened?"

"She's got *nothing-nothing!*"

"Take her into number three!"

The group hit the cubicle and split like jet fighters, each one peeling away to their post.

One nurse pressed a mask to Megan's face. "Air on..."

Another pulled away Megan's blouse, while a third pushed the small, round sensors on her chest. A fourth switched on the monitor over the bed.

Cain dropped the medical kit and swung toward the defibrillator. Dr. Harrod was already there, and he snatched the paddles from her. She didn't protest. Doctors were not supposed to be emotionally involved with their patients, but it might be the edge they needed to bring her back. Looking at the flat, green line on the monitor, she knew it would take some kind of a miracle to save Megan.

"Hurry!" Cain snapped, thrusting the paddles at intern Judie Reynolds. The young woman squeezed gel onto them and backed away. "Okay, everybody off!"

The nurse on the air bag stepped back, and Cain pressed the paddles to Megan's chest. He shot her, and her body jumped.

"Nothing!" said the nurse on the monitor. "Putting back air."

"Pupils dilated," said a third. "No response."

Cain handed the paddles to Reynolds and began massaging Megan's heart.

"Please, Meg, do something... anything."

Megan's head lolled from side to side, her face colorless, lips nearly so. Her eyes were open, and her fingers hung limply over the side of the table.

"Meg..."

Harrod laid a hand on the young man's shoulders. "Cain... Cain..."

He ignored her. She was a quitter, he wasn't. *More time.* Megan just needed more time. He continued pressing.

Harrod looked up, nodded to the nurses. The air bag was withdrawn, the sensors removed.

"No!" Cain blurted. "She needs them. Just a few more seconds!"

"Cain, we've lost her," Harrod said softly. "There's nothing more you can do."

The young man stopped pressing. He stood over her, arms locked, hands on her chest, head bowed. He was overwhelmed with guilt as he considered all the things he could have done to make this turn out differently. If they'd only taken the stairs. If he'd taken off the zombie's head first. If he hadn't lingered just that extra moment to collect West's medical kit in the autopsy room.

If.

Cain stepped back from the body.

"I'm sorry," Harrod said. She motioned the others out the door. "We'll use the other rooms... you can have a few minutes."

Judie Reynolds brushed her hand across Megan's eyes, shutting them, as she left her side. Cain acknowledged the gesture with a nod, then shook his head. He picked up the hand and rubbed the fingers slowly between his.

"I let you down," he said through tears. "I failed you tonight... and when you tried to warn me about West. You were right about him." He lowered to his knees, drew her hand to him and kissed it, put it to his cheek. "He was mad, and I didn't listen."

Megan's hand was cold. He cupped it in his hands. "Just like in wintertime" - he smiled at her - "when we'd walk through Gaines Park. I'd hold it and breathe on it and bring back the circulation."

It wasn't fair. She would be alive and well if just a part of her hadn't failed-

Cain looked up.

"Bring back the circulation..."

He looked behind him, toward the door.

If.

"If I hadn't stopped... for the kit."

No, it was insane. Yet every moment he hesitated, she slipped further away. He had none of her now. At best, she would return like Hill. At worst - at least he would have a part of her.

Leaping to his feet, he went to the kit and pulled out West's notes. He had given Hill's head 5 cc's, his body 10. He'd been dead only a half-minute. Cain thought hard. Halsey had been given 12 after a minute. Obviously, that hadn't been enough.

"Fifteen cc's for thirty seconds was enough, so four minutes..." He dropped the notebook, picked up a vial of reagent. "Four minutes should take 60 cc's."

He ran to get a hypodermic from the stainless steel cabinet and slipped it through the rubber stopper. Would 60 cc's be too much? Gruber's brain couldn't absorb 25 cc's, but he'd only been dead a few seconds.

He stopped at 60 cc's and bent over her body. "I love you, Megan. Forgive me."

Cain bunched her hair to one side, exposing the back of her neck. He put the needle to the base of her skull and jabbed it in. His breath came fast, and his mouth grew pepper dry as he emptied the needle. Pulling it out, he shut the door and once again took her hand. Over the bed the clock ticked loudly.

Five. Six. Seven seconds. He counted them out - God help him, just like West.

There were noises in the hallway, loud voices and the crackle of a walkie-talkie. Cain couldn't make out all of what was being said, but he heard that the fire was under control and that no additional help would be needed. He wondered what had happened to the zombies.

Ten seconds. Eleven. Halsey had come back at twelve.

Twelve, thirteen, fourteen...

Megan's mouth twitched, opened. Then her eyes. "Meg?" Cain said excitedly. "Meg!"

She looked at him. There was a moment of

stone silence and immobility, and then she screamed.

"Let that be a lesson to you," Vinnie Papa said from the back seat of the speeding cruiser. "When an officer's got a hunch about something, he has to follow it. Otherwise, he may be upholding the law, but he isn't doing his job."

Dave Karlin nodded as he thumped over the curb and into the Miskatonic parking lot. He pulled beside Dean Halsey's space.

Papa shook his head. "I should've booked him on something. Then *I* could've had the little killer instead of the coroner." He sighed. Ever since they'd gotten Mace's call, he'd been like a dog with a bone, railing on about West. He suspected Karlin had stopped listening after the first five minutes, but that didn't stop him from complaining. He hated losing a killer, especially when he'd known in his gut that West was the man. He didn't understand why evidence took precedence over instinct.

"Poor Halsey," he said as he climbed from the car. "I understand West got him pretty bad. Chopped off his head and everything."

Karlin burped behind his hand as he followed Papa into the hospital. There was a thin tester of smoke hanging in the lobby. Though the elevators had been shut down, smoke was creeping up the shafts and through the doors. Papa and Karlin headed for the stairwell.

The corridor outside the autopsy room was filling with smoke as the last of the fires was extinguished. Papa put his handkerchief to his mouth as he approached Captain Joe Orlando, whose black turnout coat was covered with water and blood.

"Someone hurt?"

Orlando followed his gaze to the coat and shook his head. He turned down his walkie-talkie and took a short breath from his oxygen mask. "There's blood and shit all over the place, drippin' from the walls. It's like someone painted with the stuff, you can't avoid it."

Karlin coughed behind his own handkerchief, and his cheeks went green.

"What did it, Joey?"

The portly firefighter pointed to the autopsy room. "Looks like some kind of electric drill went haywire, started toasting things."

"And the fatalities? All from the fire?"

Orlando shook his head. "Looks like there was some kind of explosion in there. There're bodies and furniture all over. And we saw the weirdest thing when we came down."

"Oh?"

Orlando took a whiff of oxygen and said, "Three men came runnin' toward us. They were spastic, retarded I guess, but strong as hell. One of 'em threw that desk around like it was cardboard. They didn't seem to understand when we yelled to get out. Then one of em picked up the door to the autopsy room and made like he was goin' to throw it, which is when we hit them full-blast with the hose. They didn't like that and ran into the room. Tore the goddamn exit door off its hinges, and that was the last we saw of 'em."

"You get a good look at them?"

"No, their faces were all cut up. But they shouldn't be too hard to find."

"Why is that?"

"'Cause the three of 'em were naked as bluejays. Spastic and naked, not too common hereabouts."

Papa sent Karlin to put out a bulletin on the men and then wiped tears from his eyes. The smoke was acrid, painful.

"Any survivors?"

"Just one that we know of. One of the medical students."

"Tall good-looking kid?"

"He was tall," Orlando said, "but that's all I can tell you. He was covered with soot and blood..."

"Where is he now?"

"Upstairs. His girlfriend was hurt."

"What about the guard?"

"Y'mean Mace?" Orlando snickered. "We saw him strolling down Kadeth with his tie loose and looking like he didn't have a care in the world. I get the feeling this was his last day on the job..."

Thanking him, the detective put his handkerchief to his mouth and entered the room. Six firefighters were trying not to disturb any of the bodies as they used a pair of canvas hoses to put out small blazes. Papa had been at Attica during the riots; this looked worse. There wasn't a cabinet or table which hadn't been smashed; disemboweled bodies were everywhere, blood and water running together in streams along the tiles. He knew at once there'd been no explosion. Blasts left burns and threw matter outward, and one strong enough to cause this much destruction also would have damaged the walls.

Nor would a blast have explained what had happened to Herbert West.

West lay near the sink, sprawled across an unidentified body. The body had been opened from chin to genitals, its viscera and bone hanging from every side. Only its intestines were intact, tangled around West's neck and torso.

He felt a certain sadness. Obviously, a trio of lunatics had escaped from the psychiatric ward and gone on a rampage. West hadn't done anything, he was merely an innocent victim. The day was suddenly dark

196

and unhappy. He looked down at Dean Halsey's head, watched as rushing water pulled licks of blood from the neck.

"It's been a bad day for all of us, huh?"

He happened to notice, then, what looked like Halsey's body nearby; he went over and crouched beside it. It would have been tough to be certain, what with the arms and head missing, but the shirt pocket was monogrammed, and he was sure the shoes were Halsey's. They were orthopedic, specially made.

They were also caked with mud, Papa was certain, from the lawn where they'd found the body of Lenny Wengler.

It was too much to believe - West innocent and Halsey a killer. He intended to grill Daniel Cain more than a little.

Feeling lightheaded, Papa took a hit from Orlando's air before heading upstairs to talk to Cain. Upon reaching the lobby he was informed, much to his chagrin, that Cain was gone. Dr. Harrod informed him that Megan Halsey's body was also gone. Papa immediately called security and ordered the hospital searched, then phoned headquarters to have squad cars sent to the Cain and Halsey homes. A half-hour later, Cain still had not been found.

All that police had discovered were the three lunatics, all of them lying dead by the side of Kadeth. One had obviously been killed by a shotgun blast to the head, another by a slit wrist, the third by some kind of vehicular accident. The reports were one thing more, which didn't make sense to Papa. Those injuries were the same causes of death listed on the tags hanging from their big toes. That meant they'd been fatally wounded long before they died.

The detective had a hunch Cain could explain it all, but after hearing about the bodies and thinking about Mace's sudden departure - the guard was lazy, but he wasn't a coward - he found himself hoping the young man stayed lost. Papa valued his sanity more than his track record and, shrugging and leaving the hospital with the queasy Karlin in tow, this was one time he wasn't sure he wanted to know all the answers.